THE MAO GAME

THE MAO GAME

A NOVEL

JOSHUA MILLER

ReganBooks
An Imprint of HarperCollins*Publishers*

Lyrics on page 184 are from "Everybody Knows" by Leonard Cohen.

HarperCollins books may be purchased for educational, business, or sales promotional use. For information please write: Special Markets Department, HarperCollins Publishers, Inc., 10 East 53rd Street, New York, NY 10022.

FIRST EDITION

Designed by Ruth Lee

Library of Congress Cataloging-in-Publication Data

Miller, Joshua (Joshua Israel)
    The Mao game : a novel / by Joshua Miller.
       p.   cm.
     ISBN 0-06-039185-5
     I. Title.
     PS3563.I41325M3   1997
     813'.54—dc21   97-5847

97 98 99 00 01 ❖/RRD 10 9 8 7 6 5 4 3 2

For Grandma

Acknowledgments

I'd like to thank the following people:

Michelle Ari, Susie Ariel, Bruno Bernard, Ruth Bernard, Cyndi Braisted, Kate Braverman, Norman Brokaw, Eve Babitz, Rob Carlson, Sylvia Cohen, Warren Cowan, Jill Cutler, Joan Didion, Carly Eiseman, Georgia Froom, David Francis, Fran di Lustro Gordon, David Groff, Jordan Gallader, Sara Gilbert, Gloria Gifford, L.R.H., Jennifer Gates Hayes, Marlene Hemmerling, Paula Susan Harris, Don Jeffrey, Kristin Kiser, Lightfield Lewis, Toby Maguire, Jason Miller, Joseph Montebello, Paul Olsewski, Linda Palmer, Les Plesko, Darrel Redleaf, Judith Regan, Gay Ribisi, Marissa Ribisi, Peter Rosenblat, Amy Schiffman, Brie Shaeffer, Angela Sharp, Sara Smith, Alex Smithline, Ilene Staple, Art Stashower, Martha Stillson, Tim Swain, David Vigillano, David Wallis, Susan Watson, Heather Watson, Walter Yetnekoff.

And most of all, my mother, Susan Bernard.

Thanks also to *Playboy* magazine, *Esquire, Harper's*, Antioch College, Yale University, and UCLA.

A regret
A single regret
makes a
doorway.
What is
a door way,
a door way
is a photograph.

GERTRUDE STEIN
WHAT HAPPENED

My mother plays a card game called Mao.

Mao was created in Chinese POW camps.

They shot everyone who didn't win.

Mother hands me a two-page booklet of rules. The cover is a picture of Mao and reads: THE RULES OF MAO. Inside the booklet is one blank page of paper.

The players have to figure out the rules as they play cards. The dealer is the dictator of the game, announcing his secret rules as a game progresses. If you are dealt an ace, your penalties could have thirty different outcomes. It could mean that you have to shoot your own mother. It all depends on the rules created by the dealer. It's very difficult to win. Up to now, my mother was always the dealer.

I watch my grandmother and mother play Mao.

"What's your prize?" Mother asks.

"Jordan gets to live with me," Grandma says.

"If I win, you won't die," Mother demands.

"We're not playing for cancer," Grandma tells my mother.

"It's a new rule," Mother says, her voice desperate.

"I'm the dealer."

"What about the ruby ring?" my mother asks.

"If you win two games out of three."

"Is that all?"

Grandma begins shuffling the deck. "Two cards for talking out of turn," Grandma says.

My mother starts to cry.

"Two cards for crying," Grandma adds.

Mother has practiced for this game for weeks, creating every new rule she could conceive for whenever she can get to deal. Mother believes she can save Grandma's life with a game of cards.

Grandma doesn't need to say much during the game; she keeps her chin up, fondling the pearl beads on her necklace, holding a glass of champagne in her left hand. This is Grandma's Monte Carlo version of poker face. Grandma has never needed a poker face. It's glamour that wins the game.

"I want to take a drive to the desert," Grandma says.

"Is this your idea of a real game?" Mother asks.

Grandma doesn't respond.

"They should put you away," my mother tells Grandma as she starts picking at her own skin.

"Go to hell."

"This is what you say to your daughter. *Don't play hard. Play light. Forget the rules.*"

"Marry rich and become a star," Grandma adds.

"What are you going to do with Jordan?" Mother asks. Queen of spades is placed on the center deck.

"We're going to take a trip," Grandma says. "He'll be mine until I die."

"Whose idea was it to have this game?" I ask, barely audible.

"Chinese who tried to play for freedom," Grandma says.

My mother places two jacks of clubs onto the center deck.

Grandma deals Mother two more cards.

"What was that for?"

"Failure to say 'Have a nice day,'" Grandma says.

My mother picks a jack of hearts on the center deck. "How long is he going to be your son?" my mother asks.

"Until I get the right picture," Grandma says, reaching for another card. Grandma places another card on my mother's growing deck.

"Why did I get a card?"

I know my mother will lose. We know how to trick in this family.

"He's my last subject," Grandma tells my mother.

Grandma wins the Mao game. It's the only time Mother ever lost a game. And this is the last time Grandma and my mother play Mao.

What if someone asks for a rematch?

As I sit in the backseat of my mother's limousine on the way to rehearsals for my film, I realize I want to go live with Grandma.

Grandma losing the game also means Grandma could die. I don't know what happens to me or this family until we play Mao.

"How do I win this game?" I ask, turning to no one in particular in the car.

I remember my tenth birthday. That's when the studios started associating me with words like *commodity. Stock.*

At my birthday Mother asked, "Don't you have any friends?" The party was in Griffith Park. We were at the horse rides.

She had sent three dozen engraved invitations to all of my friends and offered to pick them up in limousines. I never was at school because I was working on films.

That day we sat out under canopies built around the horse stables. Everywhere was the scent of eucalyptus trees. This park was invisible to the rest of Los Angeles.

I was ten years of age and I appreciated the vanishing points of Los Angeles, like Devil's Island, a lost island off the coast of South America.

At every birthday party I had, my mother had to have a cake with my picture on it, an eight-by-ten photograph of me in sugar and chocolate.

I would be passed around the party and everybody ate me. Some would take a big piece of my eyebrow, others would consume a fourth of my chin. My mother ate my eyes, vanilla beans, and chocolate for eyebrows. The remains of my face would be put into Mother's combination-locked refrigerator, and I could pretend to be freezing.

My birthday party was catered with French food, starting with baguettes, duck mousse pâté, and champagne, then endives soaked in salt and vinegar. I always imagined endives were the wings clipped from doves, laid on a bed of lettuce.

That day at my tenth birthday party, my whole fake family came from the movie I was making. The father was nicer than my real dad. I even had a girlfriend who liked me in fiction. She had gold hair in gigantic curls and her own set of flippers, a crown created for young actors who lost baby teeth. I was in a real family. They were very good people and treated me like a son. The black tuxedo I wore belonged to the studio. I didn't think this fake family would bring me anything real to my real birthday party. They were all in character. We were a family.

I had thirty friends at my birthday party, extras who played in the movie's school scenes. I didn't know their real names. Only principal numbers one, two, three, and four, or background friends. I talked to them in character, pretending we had played or went to each others' houses.

During the banquet I sat in the corner eating fruit. Citrus represented everything I loved about Los Angeles. It was something no one could take away from me. Meanwhile, I was like doll parts scattered around on people's tables and in their mouths.

The birthday cake came out and I was on fire. Ten candles surrounded my requiem cake. I looked at my edible face and the vanilla frosting smeared across my cheeks and I couldn't eat myself. I was seven layers of rum and dried cake.

"You take the first piece," Mother said, holding a piece of me in her hand with a knife.

"I can't."

"Then everyone else will eat you."

"I don't even taste like rum," I said.

3

My name is Jordan Highland. I was born a blue baby. I was dead when I was born. They had to tie my mother's insides up after she choked me.

That's not in the script, my mother would say.

This is who choked me.

My mother is dropping me off at Grandma's, to live.

In the car, I think of the women in the books Grandma gave me of Edward Hopper paintings. Alone and staring out at some indistinguishable plateau, the women in the paintings are tired, weak, drowsy; like my mother, they have skin tones painted opaque, white oils.

Their hair is always knotted with strands falling from clips and sometimes tied into buns. Are these people in the paintings Mother? Sometimes Hopper puts red tones into the cheeks, but the rest of the body is a weak flesh color and pink at the ridges. This was how I see my mother. Not what she looks like with makeup but how she was in the mornings, before she had to face herself and her son.

Mother is an actress. She is dedicated to contemplating the next move, screenplay, or character.

She's into drama. Mother is concerned about the words

and rhythm of Tennessee Williams, Eugene O'Neill, David Mamet, Edward Albee. They wrote roles she played on Broadway. She took roles in big budget Hollywood films, which made her a movie star and gave her the power to start making films based on great novels and plays. She is working on making Dostoyevsky's *Crime and Punishment* into a film.

Mother is preparing to play Queen Elizabeth I. She is a method actress. Everyday she lives in the character she plays. Mother is up at the crack of dawn to evoke the tragedy of Elizabeth's life. She aims to communicate with the dead before the sun rises.

Mother washes her face with ice and water in the mornings out of a silver bowl before she takes a hot shower. She then thinks about dialect, makeup, the size of her wardrobe. Everything she does in the morning is retribution for Queen Elizabeth I. In the last three weeks, my mother playing dialect tapes echoed through the house, the English consonants repeated one hundred times, my mother's voice making long vowels as she walked the hallways in her bathrobe, hair up in curlers and the dye setting on her head. I usually go over lines with her in her bedroom. The carpets are white, the room is spare. Fifty by fifty feet. One large red kimono is hung and framed in a glass case above the bed. Painted across the kimono in white Chinese lettering is the name Mao. Above her teakwood dressing table, there is one large framed portrait of Chairman Mao.

In the kitchen, my mother's fresh-squeezed orange juice has to be cold and fill the glass just to the rim. The vitamins are placed on the kitchen table in order of intake. Her wheat toast is laid out without any butter. No fats or unhealthy foods in the house. Sometimes, no food at all. The refrigerator is always locked. It contains only bottles of water, as if Mother were on a desert safari.

These were the habits my mother retained from her actress days in Hollywood during the sixties, when you had to be able to fit into a bikini to act. At night she would perform in dramatic plays, developing her technique and craft, practicing her elocution. In her movies, the directors wanted her in a white leather miniskirt, silver go-go boots, tangiers orange lipstick, falsies, and fake eyelashes with blue mascara, her brown hair in overgown ringlets. The studios told her to go to strip shows to learn how to sway her gait. I compare my mother to Marilyn Monroe in their attempt to not be a woman, so they could act.

We live in Hancock Park. What I love about Hancock Park is that you can find a dealer ten blocks away, past Western Avenue to Bonnie Brae. We are supplied quite well by the outside; you can reach your hand out for citrus or a bag of speed. I can get an overdose very easily, and that's consoling.

I have just started going to the smack house. I pay for these exotic proclivities by residual checks from my acting jobs and the art of stealing my mother's jewelry. I took her diamond brooch the size of my palm. For the last six months I've been getting money to get high by using an eyebrow tweezer to free the little diamonds and sell them to the Hollywood Loan and Collateral Store on Vine Street. I figure one day my mother will want her diamonds back.

I know Hancock Park by my own drug trips. I've seen the endless attempted deaths, when the ambulance rolls down the street and neighbors run to the curb, excited that something is happening, red and blue flashes on their porcelain faces. It's either the old trying to jump out of windows because they've decided they can't take the chemotherapy anymore or it's a director who got his cocaine supply cut and decided to beat up the kids and their friends.

We put up a Christmas tree every year. My mother kept our tree until Easter, so we always won the award, given by the Hancock Park Women Realtors Association, for the house that keeps its tree up the longest. Real estate brokers own most of Hancock Park. The boys in the neighborhood all go to Loyola Boys School. I applied to Loyola Boys School, but they didn't accept me. I was refused by the admissions committee. I am Jewish.

So I went to movies with Grandma or on auditions. I was going to become a big movie star; I was told that would be the best revenge.

When Grandma won me from my mother in a game of Mao, I was fifteen, Grandma was seventy-five. I was still a kid in movies, where my mother's and Grandmother's will had worked to make me a star, a small star, often playing the most violent young people ever portrayed on screen in cult films. I was the kid with the gun. However, my voice was changing and I started to get tall. And my life was changing. No role had prepared me for puberty. What I enjoyed was being other people, having other people's thoughts, living in their actions. I did not see myself as a single person but as a vessel to inhabit other people's lives. It is easier to be an object; that way you can slip into spaces and listen to the other side of silence.

I am known as the "illegitimate neighbor." On the surface of Hancock Park everybody was married. And if you weren't, you didn't admit divorce. My mother is known as Mrs. Lorraine—they couldn't bring themselves to call her Ms. Lorraine.

I could never have played football, one of the games that made parents of kids in Hancock Park esteemed. My body was thin and has no muscle and my mother told me I was not the kind to be in an ensemble. Besides, my father is a famous football player. That is more than enough reason to avoid football. Each Christmas, my father would send me Notre Dame football jackets, hats, jerseys, footballs, and warm-up suits. Late at night, as soon as I was old enough, I would burn the football uniforms in the fireplace.

When I look at Mother's house, how big does my mother's luxury have to be? My mother's house has large wood beams stretched over the living room, French windows overlooking ponds and lilies, and bedrooms with chaise longues, always pink velvet or horsehair. The mahogany is forever. The white crystal chandeliers are always burning. Money is tight but the glamour never ceases. That would be unfair. The wood floors always are polished, and the tiles and patio always swept.

Grandma's photographs hang on the walls. It's to remind my mother that she's still alive. The pictures are of men in deserts and dancing women in beaded dresses. Mother also collected Grandma's nude figure photography. Usually they are of women who stripped on Sunset Boulevard in the forties. Skin was exotic then. Mother's house was a tribute to naked women. Everything was pink, silk, and strippers.

The rose garden outlines the walls surrounding her house. When the rain falls on the burgundy and white roses, they look drenched, like showered heads, clean and immune to the characters my mother plays in the house.

When my mother picks a rose, I know she is better. She starts believing in her own worth. The sliced branch represents a move toward the next role. These roses keep her alive. When they die, she will die.

4

My mother sits in the back seat of her black limousine, her forehead creased, staring outside the window, squinting at daylight, her narrow gaze protecting her.

I try to learn everything about her in one minute. "What's wrong, Mother?" I ask.

"Nothing. I'm fine," she says. She makes a quick smile to cover the dialogue. My mother looks like she might cry. Her brown eyes dilated. I watch the black mascara, seeing if it will drip.

"I'm wonderful. My life is great," she tells me.

"Are parents always in a constant state of denial?" I ask.

Mother uses her hands to cover her mouth.

"Why do you look like you're going to cry?" I say.

"It's bad makeup," she says. Mother opens her purse and pulls out a compact. She places the powder all over her face and then applies lipstick; her tongue licks the corners. Then she places her mouth into a tissue and kisses it, softening the gloss. The bright orange lipstick contrasts with my mother's olive skin. "How do I look?"

"Beautiful," I tell her.

"We're all the same in bed when the lights are off."

"I've got to go." I grab my suitcase.

"She'll objectify you. Turn you into a picture," she says. "Everything is about her pictures. If you weren't attractive she wouldn't care," my mother tells me. "It wasn't until I was sixteen that my mother cared about me. And that's when she decided I was pretty enough to be in *Playboy*."

I reach for the door handle.

"What are you going to do?" she asks.

It's getting humid inside her car. I want to get out into dry air. "I don't know," I say.

"Hollywood can't wait forever."

"I need time to just not *know*."

"They forget easily," she says.

My mother's eyes chide me. The door won't open. When the car stopped she automatically locked the doors.

"Something will happen; you'll get hurt."

"I can take care of myself," I say. I press the button and lower the window in one movement. My mother grabs at my shirt. As I try to climb out, my shirt begins to rip down the sides, the fabric caught in my mother's nails and the car window.

"I don't want you to go," she pleads.

"I want to live with Grandma."

"Give me a chance," she tells me. "I'll be a better mother." She prods her heel into my knees and pulls me from the window and back into the car, all her strength in her grip. "I'll buy you anything you want."

I take her briefcase full of screenplays and throw it at her legs. She grabs my hair, pulling with all her might at the roots, tugging my body across the car. She grips me hard with her fists. Her whole face is wet. I can almost taste the eyeliner on her cheek when she positions her head onto my shoulders.

I quickly reach around her, click the lock, open the door, and get out.

My mother jumps out of the car and starts chasing me down Romaine Avenue. When she sees I am out of reach she throws her orange high heels with the black tips at me.

"Let's have a rematch of Mao!" she yells.

I continue running toward Grandma's apartment.

"I'll win!" she rails.

I look back once to see my mother on her knees, collapsed on the concrete, her head nodding, hands over her face, the knuckles red from pulling my hair. Mother looks like a small fire burning on the curb.

As I leave my mother in a prayer position on Romaine Avenue, I see what she must have looked like when my father left her. Father had moved to the West Coast; they wanted to put him in movies because he was a famous football player. He had three kids back home in New York and was still married. He was on the run and got my mother pregnant. He promised he would get a divorce and be a father to their child.

When my mother was pregnant with me, she had to hide the growing baby. My father told her it would look bad for the divorce trial. Mother had to wear long yellow dresses, not go out in the daylight, and in general pretend she wasn't pregnant.

In her womb I would have felt her feet, tired from running furtively to doctors' offices, the deep gut pain in her stomach, her hand covering the little bulge. The warm waters in the uterus were composed of fear, the womb itself a closet in the larger room that she hid in: the fact of Father suggesting it was getting obvious.

Mother, with me eight months inside her, drove home late one night to my father's house in Malibu. The bronze coast was a place for hiding, and it took her a half hour to find her way down Pacific Coast Highway. Fog had clasped at the water and drifted over parts of the highway, covering telephone poles and the yellow driving lanes on the asphalt.

She walked into the house and saw empty scotch bottles on the floor, rolling paper, empty cigarette cases, lace underwear that was violet and pink. She heard the deep groaning laugh of my father and his pleasures.

Carrying the baby inside her, she climbed the staircase, her feet full of corns, raw and dried from her growing water weight. She had a clear perception of the noise from the master bedroom.

Father's eyes, dilated and pink—maybe from pink-eye, since he had not been able to adjust to the Santa Anas in California—avoided her.

Later my mother sat in the living room before an open suitcase, piling in the possible objects she had accumulated for a baby boy—yellow pajamas with insulated feet, blue-and-white overalls, white shoes—and her book *The Web and The Rock*. She had been reading Thomas Wolfe's novel about a young man growing up, hoping through osmosis it would bring her a male child. She told me later how easy it would have been to give me up. She said it was an act of love that I even got born.

This afternoon on Romaine Avenue I am watching my mother on the ground, the heat making ripples in the air, her knees burning on the sidewalk, bare toes marked with tar. Her eyes stare at me through the heat wave. I see her eyes, her expression pleading, but her face and muscles become relaxed and unstiff and her forehead lines disappear. The heat has taken her away.

I keep walking. I know she thinks I'm leaving her the way my father did. I walk away to let her know that I do not belong to my father or my mother or anybody.

I am walking away still.

5

My mother never knew that I discovered on my own even deeper fissures in my father's life.

When I was eight, before our evening together, he made a gourmet dinner. From the beginning, I was accustomed to butter on the skillet, a sweet vapor throughout the house, and steam over the windows. My father knew French cooking, and he was preparing a corn-fed chicken with crayfish sauce and a soufflé suisse.

Our swimming trunks were drying out on the rails of the balcony, dusted with sand and rocks from an afternoon in the ocean. My father's house was so close to the water that at night I felt I was looking out a porthole when the tide came in and crashed against the sandbags and rocks.

He liked to feed me while we were in bed. I sat propped up against high pillows, my body lower under the covers. He held out a plate of endives in vinaigrette.

"This is all right," he would tell me. "The Puritans always made love to their children."

He placed the food in my mouth—the fresh mozzarella he grated by hand, orange tomatoes, basil on the side. I could feel the spices in my body.

"I love you," he said. "I'm so proud of you."

We ate together on Saturday evening; I was filled for the month. My father spent hours in the kitchen. He was looking to make me feel good.

"I don't make love to you on Saturday night," Father told me. "We wait until Sunday."

I would sleep with his food inside me. I looked forward to being fed by my father; all week I waited for the chance to be with him on Saturday night. He then would crawl into bed with me and hold me. I felt this was all right, the ocean reassuring me behind our back. He promised when I got older we would go to his hometown, do acid by the lake, curve it with shots of tequila and lime rinds; it would take hallucinations to make us father and son.

"I wasn't there when my father died," he told me. My father was from a small Germanic town outside Baltimore, Maryland. I've seen it once. I remember large gray stone courthouses and churches, the spires reaching up into a lampblack sky. All that was left were dead train tracks.

"When I was eighteen I built a garden for my father." My father explained to me how he dug into the gullies of his father's backyard, gorged the ground with bulbs of narcissus, roses, basil, and thyme on breaks from school and practicing on the football team. After it was built he came home and found his father lying unconscious in the garden.

I had never met my grandfather, the sailor around the world, the man who knew everything about the wind and its effects on water, but when I heard my father tell this story, I wanted him to ask me to build a garden for him.

"I want you to get your rest," he told me, placing the covers over my body.

My father would pick up a copy of Shakespeare's plays and recite monologues. I could feel the salt of the ocean next to me. He sat across from me, reading in his deep stage voice, enunciating every phrase and beat. He sometimes would hold me close to him as he read from Prospero's passages in *The Tempest*. This lasted until 5 A.M.

Those nights as he read to me at the beach, I felt the windows of my father's house were protectors. The inside of the house, all in dark Spanish bookcases and sculptures, was my father's masculine strength.

The strong odor of cedar, the cod pond, and tall grass— all meant safety. I lay safe in the pillows, warmed by the ten shelves of books and my father's cigarette smoke. I felt almost religious in this large house, each wooden doorway a passage.

6

Grandma lives in the real Hollywood. One mile south of the giant ivory-white capital letters fastened to bedrock, polished white and always glaring in the sun on the Hollywood Hills.

Once a year a letter would fall out of the Hollywood sign. Sometimes I looked at the sign backward, upside down, crooked, hoping the meaning would change with each different perspective and become a hieroglyph, like Stonehenge.

Just before she played that game of Mao with my mother, Grandma had given me a brown oak box. Inside were twelve colored lenses for the camera, lined up along a blue satin interior. Each lens was framed with sterling silver. When I held them to my eyes, I had a new eyesight for the universe.

I prefer the view only out of these lenses. Whether I am actually wearing them or not, I exchange my depth of field for the lenses and the redefining speeds of film from Grandma's cameras. My eyes see through an aperture. I placed my grandmother's round colored lenses over my eyes like spectacles. They heightened the blues I would naturally see into operatic aquas, oranges that suggested heat strokes, balanced against the toxic air and psychedelic rainbows at sunset. Colors drugged from my own taut vision.

When I saw the Hollywood sign through the scarlet lens, it was suffused with ambulances taking my grandmother to the hospital.

Grandma's apartment was on Romaine and Vine streets, ten blocks from Hollywood Boulevard and twenty blocks north of Hancock Park. I knew Vine Street already, because that's where Hollygrove Orphanage is; my mother had conscious thoughts of sending me there. My mother said it could be a good place for a time, until I settled down. Norma Jean Baker lived there before she became Marilyn Monroe.

Every time I visited my grandmother, I saw Vine Street through a cadmium yellow street lens: the disheartened Mexican-Americans selling grilled meat and salty corn on the corner; the gentlemen's bars overloaded with male prostitutes from Santa Monica Boulevard one block away from Grandma's.

The helicopter searchlights beamed down on this ghetto, looking for the next homicide, many of them inspired by the dunce Korean Mafia in their blue silk suits, who pass out Macanudo cigars and small bags of cocaine with the words BAD BOY printed in ink on the lip of the bag.

But Hollywood for me was not just the impersonal cataclysm and unnatural light. I thought Hollywood was my grandmother's tangerine-orange hair and chiseled cheekbones. She was too forthright a star for colored lenses. Always, Grandma should have had white light projected onto her face. Always, Grandma looked like a George Hurrel photograph, with strong backlights that created shadows and the Vaseline that Hurrel brushed onto the camera's lens that made the skin satin and bronzed. Grandma's eyes were hazel, suggesting amulets and hieroglyphic art.

Grandma retained an Egyptian beauty, every plane and line of her face still defined. With her elongated posture and aristocratic neck and a single lift of her chin, Grandma was a Nefertiti commanding armies to build pyramids in the desert. Hollywood was her Egyptian kingdom.

Since I was a little boy, Grandma and I had a relationship like that of Hopper and his wife: she used me as her subject. Grandma had photographed me since I was a child. In photography, Grandma painted with light, the oils in light that show me alone in laundromats. Grandma's photographs of me with my arms folded, my eyes perplexed, and my fists clenched imply that I was abandoned. In photography you get only a suggestion of what has happened.

Grandma, like Hopper, chronicles isolation and empty spaces. Not only New England homes with their peace but big cities, with women sitting and thinking in monologues under the red lights of the coffeehouse.

7

After Mother sees me walk away, I enter my life with Grandma.

I walk through the front door and find her painting her nails a ruby red in the bathtub. It's 100 degrees. She wears white rags all over her body and forehead and a pink nylon slip. Her legs are placed above the rims of the tub, her hair gathered into two ponytails that are braided at the sides, held tight by two rubber bands.

Grandma gets up carefully from the tub and starts to wash off all the sweat at the sink. A sweet smell of salt permeates around Grandma. It blends with the heat, scouring away any residue of moisture and stripping the air of oxygen. I feel as if I am wearing a plastic bag over my face gathered at my neck like a suicide's macramé.

I ignore my mother's words about Grandma. What makes me safe to Grandma is that I'm not her daughter. I'm another child who is Grandma's second chance to love.

I'm her last subject.

"I've been sleeping in the bathtub for a week," she tells me.

"Why don't you get an air conditioner?" I ask.

"It's not good to sleep with cold air." Grandma moves

boxes aside to get through the rest of the apartment. I've never seen these particular boxes before, their lids wide open and ready to be filled.

"What are all these boxes for?" I ask.

"I'm getting ready to move," Grandma tells me.

"Where?"

"They have these great trailers for sale," Grandma says. "Maybe I'll go travel around the country."

"You always say you're moving."

"I haven't found the right place," Grandma tells me.

On the table in the living room are two glass dishes of pistachio pudding. In the corner, an old metal fan in a wire cage circulates more heat in the dense space. It's the end of August and the forecast says it will be 100 degrees for a week.

"I know your mother doesn't feed you," Grandma says. "So I made you the pudding."

"She's shooting," I say.

"Doing what?"

"Making an epic."

"That's easy work," Grandma tells me. "She doesn't know real work. I know real work." She heads over to the stacks of books. "She's always been a princess."

Grandma picks up a book and passes it to me. *Edward Hopper and Lost American Dreams*. I decide right then to treasure any object Grandma offers.

"There are no free lunches," Grandma says. "If you live here we learn things. We develop our IQs." She opens to the first page of the book. And I begin to read. "No flatliners in this house," Grandma says. "Or the dead."

Some type of salvation through a three-dimensional world of illusion.

"Read the book and study his paintings and you'll learn something about lighting techniques and his poses. How they are not posed. You catch these people and paint them while they're there."

Grandma takes the cotton from between her toes and starts to wipe off the excess with polish remover, the smell splashing over her hands and excess points of red.

"Hopper caught his stories walking at night through the city," Grandma says. "I learned that when I grew up in Provence. I have a bed for you," she goes on. "It doesn't matter, I sleep on the chair." She points to her candy-striped metal beach chair that is used for a couch.

"Isn't this bad for your back?" I ask.

"I never sleep anymore."

"I'll get you a new bed."

"I don't want it," Grandma tells me.

"I have the money."

She looks at me sternly and moves boxes to the side, kicking them. "I know your mother put you up to this," she says, clearing away tall piles of coupons. "I'm not an invalid. I can take care of myself." She throws my luggage onto the single-sized bed in the living room. "Hopper never didn't paint. He always carried the canvas and brush," Grandma says. "Hopper painted the same landscape at different times of the day."

I am not quite sure why she is telling me this. So I choose to absorb everything I hear.

"Are you hungry?" Grandma asks. "I've got a steak. Twelve ounce."

"I want to go to the movies," I say.

"Every day we will go to the movies," Grandma informs me. "We have to live each moment like a painting."

She reaches behind the bureau and pulls out four long cardboard tubes. Inside are copies of Hopper's pictures. Grandma spreads them across the bed. She sits with me alongside them, pointing out details. Her gray nail file chisels the corners of her unpainted nails, scattered dust falling from her hands.

Grandma explains to me how Hopper doesn't use a black outline or any clearly defined lines for his paintings. Not like a classical painting that has separate planes. In Hopper all planes merge.

"That's how I see Los Angeles," I tell Grandma.

"It's a watercolor, it all collapses into one, like a Cézanne," Grandma agrees.

"I can see him painting your neighborhood, all the stillness," I say. I always think of Grandma's house as the space for painting, something I want to walk into that has a farther depth of field.

8

When I moved in with Grandma, it was my first day of missing school for keeps. I was often absent making movies. When I did go to school, I stared out the closed windows, the ones with the silver wires running through them like veins, like sanitarium windows.

I looked at the teachers talking, but their voices were muted. I would stare at their feet crossing from one corner of the room to another. Homework assignments were drawn on the chalkboard, notes passed out, but I didn't see the point in perpetuating the myth that I was like everyone else. I was different. So I played along until someone found out.

Last semester I was transferred into the learning disability class. I was fifteen and the English department said I couldn't comprehend literature. In the beginning of the class we read Hemingway's *A Farewell to Arms*. The teacher read the book to the class, pronouncing every word, stressing the vowel sounds of the book as if we spoke a foreign language. When the teacher discussed the text of the novel, if we answered her questions correctly, she would pass out candy-sprinkled chocolate-peanut-butter cookies.

I was given books, assignments, and lectures. However,

the teachers did not understand my problem. Even though I had a tutor on the set, I could never turn in my homework on time because of the film shoots. So the teachers at school failed me.

During my time with a private tutor I have developed my own sense of the books I was reading. It is a liberal education in the sense that I get to study what interests me most. Like Grandma. Grandma has always been my education.

9

Grandma is unable to drive because she has glaucoma. I always wondered if it had to do with her being a photographer, taking so many pictures, a type of punishment to the eyes for witnessing beauty.

She and I get the bus on Beverly Boulevard and Third Street on my day off from my movie. As we are waiting for the bus Grandma tells me about a classic by Fernand Léger, a movie created only of various geometric shapes. He also made a twenty-minute movie that was a study of cubism and reflection in which the audience watches a lemon on the screen changing appearances with different light.

"Only the French could get away with a movie about a lemon," Grandma tells me.

All this afternoon with Grandma, there is a temporary pause in time. Time itself seemed a haze around our heads, settling on the wild tiger flowers blooming behind us on the chain-link fence.

"We're going to see *The Battleship Potemkin*," Grandma says. "Eisenstein was one of the great revolutionary filmmakers in Russia."

Grandma goes on to explain how Eisenstein had contempt for the oppressive Soviet establishment, so he had to resort to comparatively abstract images to tell the truth.

"After the war filmmakers wanted the real," Grandma says.

"I don't believe in the truth," I tell Grandma. "Movies are better."

"Only if it's in black and white," Grandma says. "The shades in the gray scale are more honest than color." Grandma looks down Beverly Boulevard for a bus. "Wait until you see the scene at the Odessa Steps. It's all Soviet montage."

We get on the bus for Russia, 1905, going to the revolution.

"They used the movies to manipulate the people," Grandma says. "Stalin was a bastard."

Grandma quickly flashes her expired bus pass to the driver and gets a seat, wrapping her long brown suede trench coat around her legs. A gold chain that my father had given me hangs under her chin. Grandma uses the necklace to carry a pocket watch.

The New Beverly Cinema is the only art house theater close to Hollywood and has a direct bus line that stops in front of the movie house. The theater is one block west of the border between Hancock Park and the Mid-Wilshire district.

We take seats in the third row, with me in the corner seat so nobody unknown is sitting next to me.

When there is no sound in a movie, it allows the space to expand around my thoughts; the film becomes a muted glow, and I grow more aware of my place in relation to it, among burnt oil and empty popcorn bags, my back reclining against the old red velvet seat, bunches of cotton sticking out of the holes in the cushions, the metal feet coming loose out of the cement floor. The seats all around us are corroded metal frames, and many rows are missing cushions, like bad teeth that have fallen out. The theater has a red wool curtain draped at the sides that does not move. It hangs to the railings, half of it on the floor, barely touching Eisenstein's images on screen. This theater's age reminds me of the Egyptian Theater on Hollywood Boulevard, without the gold leaf sphinxes and black panthers with large ruby rhinestone eyes at the entrance. This theater is for private matinees.

As I sit in the theater with Grandma, I attempt to convince myself that reaching an older age, fifteen, has erased the times my father liked to take me to the movie houses when I was six or eight. Most of his life is about what happened in the dark. From him I learned the rules of film watching.

On Friday nights, we went to the Malibu Colony Theater. I rode in my father's steel gray '64 Porsche down Pacific Coast Highway while he was drunk.

The interior of the car smelled of scotch and black leather. The windows were tinted, so nobody could see what he did. I felt I was in a spaceship and we were going to Mars.

My father drove seventy miles an hour down Pacific Coast Highway, which has four lanes, no streetlights, and is twenty yards from the shoreline. I thought we would drive off the road, into the Pacific. From where I was buried low in my seat, my eyes tagged the telephone poles as they passed, anchor points along the curved highway.

I rolled the car window down and listened to the cicadas off the highway. I knew they had been trapped underground for years and decided the season to come out. They would die within three months aboveground. I heard the voice of the male locusts singing for what is one last summer. I felt they were singing because they were happy.

Perhaps I was a cicada. I wondered how long I could live in my father's summer. Would he grow tired of me like his football at the end of a bad season?

He shoved more scotch down his throat. He upended it and held it like a football, the bottle half empty, saliva marks around the spout, the label ripped off at the sides. He then stashed what was left of it in the glove compartment, alongside the other half pints.

As we sat in the movies he would play with me. Father used his hands. I had a bowl of popcorn in my lap, my fingers drenched in salt and butter, eating all the way down to the uncracked kernels. Father reached over and moved the bowl of popcorn out of my lap and placed it on the floor. I could hear the plastic touch the floor, scratching against the concrete, and during that time I concentrated on the moving images and the empty space between my hands, left alone and waiting for something to arrive. I felt hands move over to the center of my body. Father began unbuttoning the small round copper-penny buttons on my corduroy jeans. I did not move until his hands made their way into my pants. I squirmed against his cold fingers, tracing his fingers back and forth along the rim of my stomach. I wanted to reach for the popcorn. When he grabbed the center of me, I felt a nauseous tingling churning in my back and throat. My rib cage tightened, as if I were preparing for some collision or whiplash. I kept eye contact with the light on the projector in the booth, my head turned toward the back of the theater, seeing the frames of film motored over the silver belt on the projector, trying to not look below myself.

When I came, there was just a sensation of a needle being poked into a hot balloon. My body started to sweat, and I was dizzy with the scorching feeling of peeing blood.

My father put my body parts back into my pants.

Padding them with safety. He placed the popcorn back into my lap, and he sat back reclining into the movie theater. And so did I, concentrating again on the screen in front of me. The only thoughts I had were about the origins of secrets and nakedness, of my father's hands inside me. I knew to lock them inside an imaginary vault, the way I knew Grandma protected her negatives of movie stars.

He liked movies and it was usually a bad movie. No audience. It occurred to me as we sat there why Father only liked the last row of the theater. Nobody saw in the back of the movie house and he would never go to jail. I thought about them taking him away from me while I watched the movie. That night, I hoped the doors of the theater would swing open like a million flying magnets of steel. I thought about medieval tortures. They could starve him and give him one hundred lobotomies and bury him alive.

I wanted to place all the costumes I wore for him—the underwear, lilacs, carob milkshakes, red dresses that we used, and bedsheets—around his body and light a match. I wanted his last smell to be of singed lilacs and scratchy lace underwear.

Later my father would pass out in the house, his head and body dug into the feathers, burnt cigarette holes along the tips of the sheets and pillowcases, his last drink on the bedside table, a milkshake with honey, yogurt, and a shot of vodka.

Outside my father's house, I stepped into the murky green watered ocean, letting the brine encircle my feet, shards of rocks under the toes, and I looked at the coastline, looking like the fluids that washed out of me in the movie, the crescent moon a bare profile of a body somewhere over the ripped canvas of this last frontier of the West. And I looked for a tide that took away your sins.

*　　　*　　　*

After the movie is finished, Grandma and I talk in the dark-lit theater, the yellow hues on the walls set dim, draining the color out of our skin. A scarlet pallor shades out our conversation.

Grandma asks me what I think the characters in the movie literally said; she says to translate with my imagination.

"I think they want food and freedom," I tell Grandma.

"I'll make an apple pie," Grandma says.

"I want more than food."

"All you need is to eat and sleep." Grandma moves up the aisle to the outside of the theater. "The rest is drama."

"Isn't every society's survival based on food?"

"Only in third world countries," Grandma tells me. "Here it's glamour."

Now that the lights had risen I was remembering mostly the Odessa Steps scene. The town of Odessa was revolting against the military. On the fifty steps, children and mothers were running for the battleship *Potemkin*, where the men of the families had revolted. Three hundred Czarist cavalry soldiers opened fire. Within minutes, ladies holding their babies in black shawls were falling down, not fast but slowly. A baby carriage was rolling down the steps, jump cut with the rifles being pulled and jump cut again back to the falling baby carriage. Each frame stretched out like wax. The audience never finds out what happened to the baby carriage. This was what Grandma called a story with a modern ending.

When I watched the movie, I saw Grandma on the steps, interspliced with the Soviet soldiers. She was running for the baby carriage, bodies passing out in her path, all of it in black and white. Inside the baby carriage was cancer.

I avoid leaving the theater. The stark outside, almost stripping away the cornea, the sailors on the *Potemkin* with black-and-white striped cotton shirts calling for a revolution at the sight of maggots in the meat.

In the middle of real heat outside the theater I want to be back in the cold blackness of the theater, where temperatures do not exist.

While looking down La Brea Avenue, Grandma and I could survive, because we share modern endings. We hope not to know what is going to happen. And just with that knowledge, things become more bearable in California.

10

"Jordan Highland," my mother says again, loud, over the phone.

"I'm not going." I stare at my teeth in a mirror in Grandma's apartment. "My teeth are fine."

"They need bleach," Mother says. "All that smoking."

"I don't smoke."

"Whatever you do with your teeth," Mother says. "What do you do with your teeth?"

"I don't do anything with my teeth."

Dr. Curtis was the dentist to the child stars; he had an office on Sunset Boulevard, where you went for new teeth and bleach.

Every bone in my body was x-rayed and demoralized. At eight years old I needed two new front teeth. I needed "flippers," mock teeth.

Dr. Curtis would create flippers and connect them by wire to my gums to fill the gap. My gums would bleed from the pain. I had to work. I'd cover up the holes.

Every mother showed up with her toothless child, begging for a miracle and a commercial, waiting for a child who didn't have the teeth for it.

In Dr. Curtis's office, mothers compared balance sheets

with each other. They talked about returns. How they would hide money from the IRS.

Everywhere in the office Dr. Curtis and his cohorts drilled inside children's mouths, excavating, placing bubble gum and raspberry onto wet gums. It was plastic surgery on the mouth. I was there for the nitrous.

Surgical staples were pinned all around my mouth. They punctured my skin with numbing juice, and I was full of mercury and dry gums, unable to move.

Afterward, I would get sour cherry lollipops. My reward was cavities.

My speech became slurred because of the metal in my mouth. I developed a lisp because of flippers. I went to a speech coach for my impediment. In twelve weeks, I corrected my breathing and vocal patterns. I lost the lisp. The doctors wanted autographs.

"Why?" I used to ask my mother.

"Your margins are up," she said.

11

After I give in and go to Dr. Smith, I go see Grace, the girl who works at the Deja Vu Strip on Hollywood Boulevard. I am dating her. Or maybe we're going steady. If it counts, I pay to talk to her.

Grace is sixteen and moved to Hollywood from Seattle. She has bobbed brown hair that curves around her cheeks, pale white skin, and she always wears fire-engine-red lipstick. She says she's Cherokee. She is about five-six, so we're the same size. It's a good start.

She had told me if I want to know who she really is I should read *Gone With the Wind* and *The Fountainhead* by Ayn Rand. I've never gotten the books.

Every Thursday afternoon I go see Grace.

This is what happens:

I give thirty dollars to talk to her in the back room used for lap dancing.

She says, "When are you moving out?"

"I'm living with my grandmother. She's dying."

"What's wrong?"

"Cancer."

Grace is indifferent to that news. Cancer is something

distant to her. It doesn't have to do with her job, which is to give me a lap dance.

She gets down on her knees. Below her bustier she is wearing thin black lace underwear and, farther below that, spiked patent-leather shoes. She starts to move her palms up and down my knees, each time getting closer to my groin.

"What is it?" she asks.

"I want a real date."

"It costs more."

"Okay," I say. "Where do you want to go?"

"Church."

"Where is it?"

"It's in Echo Park," she tells me. "Pick me up here."

"Sunday?"

"Yes."

"What time does church start?"

"Ten-thirty A.M.," she says. "Let's take it slow."

"I don't drive."

"How do you get around?"

"Taxis." I can't tell her I am not old enough to drive a car. "I'll get a good hotel room."

"How old are you?"

"I'm eighteen," I lie.

"I'm twenty."

That's how old she tells me today. It changes. Every time I see her, she gets younger. I realize the closer she comes to telling her real age, the more I have a chance.

12

I know how to get up early in the morning. I learned this from my mother.

My call time is 7 A.M.

We are shooting in Northridge, California, which is the last stretch of the San Fernando Valley.

People who live in the valley are losers, Mother said to me.

The valley is filled with actors—especially actors under twelve who live and commute to and from the valley for commercials and television interviews. They are separated from Hollywood by a mountain.

When I was a child, everything in my life was about how to get there, to the valley. We used residual checks for gas. All money was invested in the next possible job. The answering machine. A new look.

At seven years old, I started doing commercials and guest appearances on TV shows. I learned the timing of sit-coms. I was learning dialogue. Three-camera shows. It's not about acting, it's speed and memorization. Multiplication cards with words. It's never been about acting.

Most TV networks thought I was too "weird" to be in a

family on TV. They said I was too intense. They said I wasn't made for ensembles. I didn't fit.

It's the separation from day players and stars, my mother said about the valley.

Mother didn't like to travel. We commuted from Hollywood through Laurel Canyon to the San Fernando Valley when I had an audition. Mother called them meetings. We took bottled water and music tapes and wore shorts.

My mother avoided these cities in the valley: Woodland Hills, Encino, Chatsworth, Reseda, Northridge.

You can get cholera in the valley, Mother remarked.

I wake up at 5 A.M. and get dressed for the shoot. I look through Grandma's kitchen window at the bleak overcast white sky. I think at these times I will never see a clear day. These days look like funerals.

I walk past Grandma, who is doing yoga in the center of the living room. Grandma is in the middle of standing on her head.

"You can get hurt," I tell her.

"It's good for my heart. It thins the blood."

Retaining my mother's habits, I take seven different vitamins and a protein shake. I spike it with vanilla extract I found in Grandma's kitchen cabinet.

"Where were you last night?" she asks me.

"I'm dating this stripper."

"Do you love her?"

"It costs more, she told me."

I reached over to my backpack for the set. I place an Edward Hopper picture book, a bottle of Vicodins, a highlighter, and my script inside.

"Where does she strip?"

"The Deja Vu."

"Is she good?" Grandma asks.

"I'm in love with her," I told Grandma. "If it counts."

"What's her name?"

"Grace," I say.

"I don't trust the name Grace," Grandma says. "Be careful of women with the name Grace."

"She ran away from home," I say. "I think she could become a movie star. She reminds me of when Marilyn was Norma Jean."

"Don't let her come between you and your work," Grandma says. "You're going to become a star."

"I just want to get laid."

"Obviously," Grandma says.

As I head for the door, I start running lines in my head. These are the lines for the death scene I will play today.

"Do you know how to give a woman head?" Grandma asks. "They love it for hours."

"I don't think I'm that good."

"You better start learning."

"How?"

"Ask her to teach you," Grandma tells me.

"I agree." I contemplate having my head nestled in the thighs of Grace. "I need to learn how to give head and I want to learn how to salsa."

"Salsa takes many years."

"What about head?" I ask.

"One night," Grandma tells me.

I open the door to dawn.

"And don't let anyone upstage you," Grandma tells me. "Make sure you get the closeups."

I walk out of Grandma's back kitchen door to the driver waiting at the curb. The street is empty except for the young Mexican girls in pink and white lace party dresses carrying their lunch pails on the way to the Vine Street elementary school. Following the girls are coteries of six-year-old boys with crew cuts who wear wife-beater shirts and baggy blue pants tied loose with ropes. Their parents have sent them in early for breakfast before they go to their early jobs.

Inside the car I have twenty minutes until we arrive in Northridge. I read over my lines. I have written in the margins of the screenplay various notes. They were my pieces of business. When I arrive on the set it looks like an unintentional carnival, with all the loose trailers, generators, and giant lights hanging down from the sky; it looks like God is setting the light for the scene.

There is a cool rush that settles in from the moment I step out of the car into the frantic movement of all the assistant directors, walking around carrying walkie talkies hooked up to earphones. They have no concept of time. There is no real time on a movie set. We make time. They create night to look like day—although it's always obvious because the sun rays are coming from the east and west at the same time.

I have been making a movie where I play a vampire trapped in a child's body. My family is supposed to be white trash vampires. I have seen the molding the special effects crew did of me. It is for a scene where I am going to be burned by the sun. I looked at the statue and felt that I, not the wax body, was the object. I almost saw myself trapped in the statue, stuck in one position, disabled. It sat in the corner, its face averted. I wasn't able to touch it. I was afraid of the resemblance, the possibility that I could be cloned without chromosomes and wrapped up like the Egyptians, my skin preserved. The heart would be removed, because they believed that's where the soul was; they would save the heart and scatter its pieces in sacred areas.

In one scene where I blow up I have to begin by looking like I'm on fire. They use my original body for this, not a wax model. They build a smoke machine attached to my face, planted under a thick fake patch of skin. The hoses are connected to machines that are going to pump smoke out of my skin. For smoke they use twelve Havana cigars; they tell me it's thicker, looks more real. Then they place baking soda all around my face and spray it with water, so it fizzles, and then I go in front of the camera, with my hoses attached to the Havana cigars.

Today I am sitting in the makeup trailer. In the scene we're shooting today I get run over by a Mack truck and survive.

The makeup artist is placing cold water mixed with base onto my face. My body twitches in the chair; however, I have learned to find a direct point in the mirror to focus my attention. Blood made of corn syrup is smeared all around my temple and cheeks.

They add dirt and gravel to my face. I watch myself turn into an accident victim.

All I have to do now is act like I got hit by a truck.

13

Sunday I pick up Grace in my mother's limousine. We are in the car going to her choir practice at the church on Wilshire and Virgil. She says this is where God talks to her.

"Where did you get the car?" she asks.

"My mother."

"Who is she?"

"A mother," I say. "Diana Lorraine?"

"Never heard of her," Grace says. "What does she do?"

"She's an actress."

"I can't stand actors."

"Me too."

Grace rolls down the window and lights a cigarette. She passes me an open tiny gold box. "Do you want some?" she asks.

"What is it?"

"Poppy seeds," Grace tells me. She opens my palm and slowly drops the brown dust into the center.

I made a horizontal line, folded a five-dollar bill the way they do in the movies, and inhaled. "I've never done it before," I lied.

"It's easy," she said. "You'll get used to it."

All the way to the church, Grace and I share the last remaining drags of her cigarette. Staring through the window I saw churches in Echo Park placed like minimalls. They are everywhere. Around every corner and you slam into the Virgin Mary. She carries a child.

"I never see that in Hollywood," I say.

"In my family's religion we don't have one God," Grace tells me. "Just the light."

"Do they speak a different language?"

"Not anymore," she says. "Only in prayers. Do you speak another language?" Grace asks.

"I learned French in elementary school. My grandma is teaching me how to order food in French."

"Nobody speaks that around here. Only Spanish." Grace throws the remains of tobacco out the window. "In school the principal wanted me to learn shop, so I could have become a maid or something."

"I have two hundred and fifty-eight absences," I say.

"They wanted me to pass shop or I'd be kicked out," Grace says. "I wouldn't let them get to me. I became invisible."

"I don't even go to school," I tell her. "And my grammar is really bad."

The car stops at the corner of Sunset Boulevard and Echo Park Boulevard. The church we go to is called St. Joan of Arc.

As we walk I ask Grace why we are going to a Catholic church if she is Cherokee.

"It's to keep in touch," she tells me.

"My mother's Jewish and my father is Catholic," I tell Grace. "I didn't know you could be two religions at once."

"My parents met in the sixties at some nudist colony in Seattle. My father's Cherokee and my mother is a member of Children of God. I don't know how they met. It must have been a collision or something." Grace adds, "A plane accident."

"I think they all must be wrong about God. He must have passed them all by," I say. "He's taken his Bible somewhere else."

"There is no way he's at Joan of Arc. He didn't even save her," Grace says. "That's not religious."

"That's a hoax on us all," I say.

"Where is he now?" Grace says.

"They say he's in you."

"The only thing I feel in me is something rugged. A switchblade cutting organs into geometric shapes and tossing them out," Grace tells me.

The next Sunday Grace and I are downstairs in the rector's office. The rooms are cool on the lower floors, like Christ's body is being stored down here or it's to make you feel guilty. I touch a wall and it feels like cold snow.

Grace peers out between the door and frame and asks me to follow her.

Grace begins to undress me. I could dream in these rooms. I could feel satin enter my body and yellow roses drip from the sky, then the thought of blood. I place my hands down my pants. I start to take my pants down and feel the cool vileness of my naked body. My body is pink and undefined.

When I take off my clothes you can tell everything about me. My knees tell you I can't run, my shoulders suggest no father. No football practice as a child to build the shoulders. I slip off my socks and they stick to my toes. Black crust lives between them. I smell of tap water and mildew and need glasses, but I keep on squinting.

I hear zippers going somewhere. I know nausea is born in little rooms at the bottoms of churches.

I turn around and see Grace down to her knees. I thought, How can I forget this room? I think of us as the prophets stripping.

Grace's full rounded breasts, the circumference of my palms, she naked in front of my face as she begins to take part of me inside her mouth.

The window is ajar. From outside comes the smell of the hands of the Mexican mothers and grandmothers rolling mole with their hands on gray rocks, the butter and grease on the grill, onions, fresh red and green peppers, and tortillas.

Men with large round bellies and short stout legs, wearing straw sombrero hats, hold bottles of beer over the ledges of their apartment houses. They are staring at their past. Maybe it is the baby-blue inflatable pools that catch their attention. Or it's the seven-year-old girls in pink terry-cloth bikinis, pink patent leather sandals, and delicate painted toenails.

What I see happens at one thousandth of a second. If a camera were here the shutter would open and close quickly and silently, not open long enough for anything to remain.

.

14

A week later on the movie shoot, they load my second self with dynamite. I look at my body, my other self, on the deserted highway where I am supposed to incinerate. It is me, with all the right wardrobe. They want to keep me far away from watching me blow up. I want to be right there in front, to see myself explode.

I watch from a distance, behind wooden trenches. The camera is up close, protected in a wooden case.

From afar, I see the counting. Then my molding begins crouching over, about to fall into the ground. I see the aquiline nose, parts of my clothes, soles from my shoes vanish in the air.

"What is the nature of evil?" I ask Grandma that night in her apartment.

"The movies," she tells me.

15

Grandma and I create a vegetable garden outside her steps, planting nearly fullgrown tomato plants and spinach. The vitamins in green plants give her more time. I wrap tiny fences around the plants.

At dusk I take a walk while Grandma is preparing to take my picture. She wants an interior sitting with light stands and flashes.

The streets are empty, abandoned red tricycles on the curb and overturned into the street. The apartment complexes are sticking out their Christmas lights, the large primary-colored bulbs hanging from porches. I often wonder why Christmas lights are never removed. I think people forget they are there. Or families have packed up and left because something happened and the apartment is deserted. These lights represent what people do with children, making them ornaments, a talking fixture, left over and forgotten.

The leftover Christmas lights also suggest the lack of any religion particularly sheltering Los Angeles. Christmas in Los Angeles is more of an act of decoration, not a unifying religious thought. People move to Los Angeles to get away from God.

I look at the cases of beer and tequila on the curbs, adjacent to the pickup trucks. On the front porches of the houses are assorted pipes and game food. Behind the metal cages are chickens, roosters, and rabbits. The impoverished in Hollywood are living in circumstances similar to the villages of third world countries, where you sleep three families in a hut, save the grains, and make clay pottery, except here you get a driver's license.

I stare through the wire fence on Romaine Avenue, detached from the pre-Christmas fiesta. Men with black nets over their hair, greased back, are wearing tank tops and baggy blue cotton pants. Some even wear zoot suits. Their arms are tattooed with Celtic knots, pythons, Chinese dragons.

On Romaine Avenue, it will be more religious and violent than the Christmas celebrated in the rest of Los Angeles. Christmas will be celebrated on the curb and in the streets. For boys my age, Christmas is not about the presents to be unwrapped. It's the time of the year to join a gang. The ritual cutting. One knife across the chest tattooing the surname of the gang, and you're accepted. Wear tall white socks, low cut sneakers, and a net. Good presents are things made out metal: a .22, cocaine vial, and barbells.

I walk past neon green and lavender low-riders parked on the grass. They remind me of the toy cars I had as a child, with the spray-painted facades and the burnt orange flames over the grills. A silver engine beneath the hood.

My grandmother's '64 T-Bird is parked at the curb in front of Grandma's building, another toy car come to life. The beige canvas roof is ripped at the sides. The corner smoking windows are bashed in and pasted with pictures of Audrey Hepburn to cover the air pockets. The car sits under two flowerless jacaranda trees. I look at them with apprehension. In spring they squander one million violet petals on the roof of Grandma's car and a moist smell of mildew.

I see my mother in a car like that. That was when they taught her to always smile. They arranged her under lights to accentuate her cleavage, the most necessary dimensions for the portrait photographers, who pinned women up in *Playboy*. I have seen my mother in these pictures. I have seen her in *Playboy*. She told me she did it for the revolution, that people needed to see a woman's body, the wind under the skirts, the strong vents.

Grandma took the pictures. Maybe that's when they stopped understanding each other; perhaps it had to do with nudity. Her eyes grew estranged watching her daughter naked, exposed to the lens.

When I saw my mother naked, it was what I expected. It was not my mother I looked at but a woman whose body I already had shared. I fell back into infancy, when I looked at her naked in the picture, seeing the parts of her body I had explored as a child, when I was safe in the bedroom, our clothes on, and she was there, embodied, tolerant of me.

People tell me about these complexes young men have for their mothers. All I know is, my mother never let me sleep alone. Twelve A.M. and she would wake me up to sleep with her. It was always stuffy in her bed, the comforter pulled way over my head, and I lay unable to breathe, my mother with her arms all across my shoulders. I always looked for the edge of the bed, away from the center of my mother's body, toward the cool air drifts at the corners. My hands stretched out and clasped at the cool parts of the bedsheets.

It was like my parents were having a romance through me. I was some tunnel that stretched down Pacific Coast Highway from my mother's house on the beach all the way to my father's clapboard house on the sand. Each one used me as a pill to swallow. I was the brown chipped rocks in the foil, the spike, maybe even the methamphetamines. I was a piece of the exchange, a dropper, a vein shot. They got the kick.

When my father stopped giving her money, Mother went into withdrawal. I got the purple bruises on the ankles, blotched marks on the back, lost teeth, sprained index fingers, and I lived under the threat that I would be given up to the Hollygrove Orphanage.

That summer my mother was looking for ways to give me away. I picked up the signs early and studied my survival techniques. I contemplated my choices. I could make money as a slave. I could do child pornography. I could act in movies. To act and be great; I realized that was a way no one could give me away. Acting became the survival technique.

Six P.M. and I sat outside the school front doors, waiting to hear the car motor, the '62 black Mercedes convertible. I speculated it had broken down, blown up, or that maybe she decided to call it quits and hop on a plane to Chile. Perhaps I would get postcards. Or maybe a pocket of time had swallowed her up, an invisible black hole, and my mother could not be traced because she had tripped into infinity. Each strand of her hair was now airborn millions and millions of light-years away, part of her small body floating, and she would write me from the solar system, tell me how green everything was and that people lived off algae.

My mother did arrive for me that day. A few days later she drove by the Hollygrove Orphanage on Vine Street and Fountain, ten blocks from our house in Hancock Park. Vine Street was the end of America, a large vapid street with gas station signs lit up at the corners, the tall metal diesel company names on poles.

That afternoon, Los Angeles still looked like a small arid town somewhere north of Vegas. My nine-year-old height in the passenger seat of my mother's car barely let me see over the dashboard. It was during the end of August, when people are murdered and mothers are contemplating aborting their children, heat completely melting out rationality at 100 degrees. In the car my mother had a wet rag tied across her forehead, and I kept my head tilted out the window, trying to catch a breeze.

That afternoon, breathing was an act of hyperventilation. In the car, Mother constantly drove slowly by the orphanage, for the twenty-eighth straight afternoon that month. I was counting the numbers, contemplating if it would be an odd-numbered or an even-numbered day that I would be abandoned. During those four weeks, she had a set of my clothes packed in one black piece of luggage in the back seat—just in case.

In the car my mother reached over for her fiftieth cup of black coffee. "These things are giving me a headache," she said. "Feel how fast my heart is racing."

While my mother made a sharp left turn she pulled my head over to the center of her chest and nestled it fiercely into her red satin blouse.

"Do you hear it?" she asked. "Is it still beating?"

I came up for air.

"I don't hear anything," I told her.

"I must be dying," she told me. Mother feigned her death at the wheel. Grabbing the steering wheel hard and slowly, she casually let all the muscles in her body go. When the light turned green, she woke up. "I do great death scenes," she told me. "You don't have to worry about death," she said. "Not until you hit ten years old."

"I'm nine years old."

"I thought you were five," she said.

"I was five four years ago."

"Are you sure?"

"Don't you remember when I was born?" I asked.

"I have a really bad memory. All those drugs they gave me."

"How old are you?" I asked my mother.

"That's not public information."

Inside, the car was like being in a heat bubble. I pulled at the white threads from the leather seats with my fingers. The dashboard oak wood was buckling from the heat; the tiny knobs made of white porcelain that belonged to some part of the car were missing. I turned on the radio and listened to the static, hoping for some station to come through. The door handle on the side of the passenger door was hanging by a few screws, the leather seats hard, crackling with each movement. The door was never really closed, and I thought I could fall out.

"Hollygrove won't be permanent," my mother continued. "It could just be a temporary place until things calm down. Until I can support you. Until I work again."

My mother's eyes flirted from the rearview mirror to the two side mirrors. From her expression driving, it was as if she had decided a camera were attached to the front windshield.

"Look at my eyes," she said. "I've got crow's feet." Mother began pulling back the skin and stretching it tightly with her hands. "Actresses with crow's feet don't get good close-ups," she said. "Without close-ups, there is no performance."

I saw my mother's eyes on the outside mirror, and I saw her lips on the center rearview mirror, and I saw her thoughts and me on the outside mirror to the right where I sat. I got to watch parts of my mother in all four corners of the car. And they were all different.

The center mirror featured her lips; it was where I had

to be the husband. Being up late at night and turning down the bed, folding back the sheets and locking the doors, and combing out the dead hairs in her long red hair with the platinum Victorian sable brush.

The outside rearview mirror held my mother the artist. Maybe a painter who had hidden canvases, secret painting brushes, and a studio somewhere where she painted like Georgia O'Keeffe: pollinating tulips, Aztec skies.

Hollygrove was surrounded by a brick wall and large cypress trees. I saw a silver slide sticking out from above the trees. An ice cream truck was parked outside the orphanage, playing carousel music and selling rainbow snowcones, rock candy designed like gargantuan wedding rings that you put on your married finger, and pink smooth sherbet popsicles in the shape of a foot that had a round big toe with a gumball in the center.

On that twenty-eighth day my mother parked her car and strode through the entrance in the brick wall and up the steps. She grabbed my hand and pulled me up the steps, my small feet and toes keeping up with her quick movement. My mother was small, maybe five-two, but fast. As we climbed the stairs, my vision blinded by streaks of gold sunrays piercing through the trees, I was not resisting. I was relinquishing my future to my mother.

Inside, she demanded a tour. The dining room was decorated with wood paneling, the large round tables set for dinner with white empty plates above the knee-high wicker chairs. I thought about the idea of eating and sleeping with other anonymous boys, left behind, and my mother twenty blocks away. She would change her mind, I considered, and come back for me. Regret leaving me off with one suitcase to remember her by.

"They get up at six A.M. and have chores." The guide carried around a ruler and pointed at things curtly.

"My child doesn't bus tables," Mother said.

The guide explained that most of the kids were Salvadoran or Mexican-Americans, that I would learn Spanish and teach my friends English. "Nobody wants a kid who speaks with an accent," the director of the orphanage said.

The orphanage halls were empty, and my mother's eyes scanned the rooms, the walls bare and absent of color. I don't think she didn't drop me off because of me, but because of the lack of decor. Mother asked why I had to share a room. She didn't like the idea of bunk beds. I could fall out if I slept on top, tumble on someone, and catch a disease, she said.

As she interviewed the lady with the ruler, I contemplated the idea of starting a new life. I could create my own age, last name, and history. I could have pretended I was the son of a movie actress, and that when she became famous she would come back for me, wearing big dark cat glasses, a white silk shawl over her hair, a mole glued on with spirit gum, and whisk me away in a forties black Cadillac. And they would have paparazzi taking pictures of my mother loving me.

Or I would be a forgotten child at the swing set, on time for dinner, sleeping with other boys who waited for mothers to come back.

That day when I left the orphanage I watched my unknown roommates, gathered together and staring at me from the bedrooms, barely reaching the windows, the eyes suggesting they were looking through chicken wire.

I compared the length of my long brown hair with bangs to the other boys. My mother decided that I should resemble a classic style, maybe Louis XIV, and my hair had never been cut short. The boys at the orphanage had their hair short and buzzed at the sides. My mother saw me notice them. "Lice," she said.

They were free to get their hair cut short and be free of parents because of wars in Panama, El Salvador, Guatemala. As my mother started her car, I told them silently that I would come back. That we were all children with our own packed luggage.

16

When I visit my mother on the set, I am her dresser, her line reader, her secret director. It's 6 A.M., a cold morning in Valencia, California. The movie set is tucked neatly into the various San Gabriel mountains. I watch her shadow silhouetted against the front windshield of the Winnebago. Her reflection is the shape of her hair in Velcro curlers, her profile a shade of green from a face mask. She wears a white terry-cloth robe with her initials embroidered in blue satin across the left breast pocket. Steam rises in front of her face from her morning coffee. The only thing audible in this trailer is the nail file moving crisply across my mother's nails.

I know she has her script in a leather-bound case. She is reading each short scene with a long glance. I sit tightly into the cushions on the bed, my head dug deep into the morning. The film I shoot has a day off. It's the only time to memorize dialogue.

"Did you memorize your lines?" I ask.

"I like to improvise," Mother says. "The director is so coked up he'll never know." She walks over to the couch. A brown mink coat and other wardrobe items are hanging over the seat. I can see the water bottles placed strategically at every corner of the room. She places a blue pillow high on the couch to prop up her back. As my mother reclines back into the couch, all her weight against the pillow, a shaft of white light makes a shadow across her cheeks, which look like marble in the morning light.

She reaches her left hand out towards me. "Do my hands," Mother asks. "Can you crack that knuckle harder?" My mother's eyelids slightly close when I move her knuckles around. She watches me. "This is the only time I can be a mother," she tells me.

I pick up a bottle of moisturizer on the floor. I take her loose small hand and begin to massage the ointment on her fingers and in the clefts of her hand. I move the root of her thumb around simultaneously while I wiggle the tip of her pinkie.

"Why are your eyes so dilated?"

"We had late-night shoots." I clear my throat. "It's nothing."

"Nothing?" my mother repeats. "You look like a vampire."

I concentrate my eyes on her hands, watching my fingers mix with her skin.

"Who got you hooked?" she asks.

"I've worked twenty-hour days." I pause, keep my head and eye contact low. "Maybe it's a good idea?"

"I'll disinherit you if you use junk," she tells me. "I'll throw you out on the street." She gets up to change behind the silk screen.

I sit on the stool, my hands gripped tightly together. The shot nerves in my body make my arms and legs shake. I look at my hand, which I can't keep still. It's like a moving object in a photograph, out of focus. I get up and follow my mother to the silk screen. Her bare back is to me.

"It's not that Grace?" she asks.

"We're just friends."

"Am I going to lose you to her?"

"Eventually," I say.

My mother is dressed and moves to sit down in front of the makeup mirror.

"Have you slept with her?"

"No," I say.

"You can tell if she's a slut if she's really wide," my mother says. "Don't sleep with her if she is." Mother picks up her lipstick and begins testing the red ocher color on her wrist. "Are you gay?"

"Not all," I say.

I stare at my mother in the mirror. In the reflection my head is resting on her shoulder. My eyes look dimmed and exhausted. These are the times that I remember having a sexuality for other purposes, when I intended sex for a high or to become a father, and in this moment I think my mother knows what happened to her son.

"Maybe I want to save her," I say.

"That's outdated," she tells me. "What's it like to kiss her?"

I moved around on the chair, adjusting the weight, avoiding answers. "It goes real slow," I say.

"If she got you hooked, I'll have her murdered," my mother informs me. There is a knock at the front door of the trailer. It's the ten-minute warning.

Mother lies back into the seat. "I'm tired of being Wonder Woman."

"What else would you do?" I ask.

"I don't even know what I'm doing now," she tells me.

17

After having spent twelve hours with my mother, I am looking for Vicodins.

Inside Grandma's apartment I'm experiencing the last remnants of Indian summer, the bronze skies and blemished clouds suggesting winter. I saw this through the colored lenses, wrapped around my eyes, held tightly and cupped by my cheeks.

Tonight, I'm searching for a fix. I know Grandma has morphine in her pill bag. While Grandma talks to me through the bathroom door, I go through her small maroon makeup bag in the medicine cabinet.

"How was the movie?" Grandma asks.

"My mother won't memorize her lines," I say. No prescription drugs in her makeup bag.

"She's dyslexic," Grandma tells me.

"How do you know?" I yell.

In her purse on top of the toilet tank I find three orange bottles with childproof tops. I jam the caps open and pour the painkillers into my palm. They are small and feel cool on my fingers.

"She can't spell," Grandma says. "And she's anemic."

"How do you know?"

"She was anemic since she was a child," Grandma says. "Look at her gums. White. And she's always tired."

"Can it worsen?"

"And she drinks too much coffee," Grandma says, ignoring me. "All that caffeine in her body could destroy her organs. And she's always shaking."

I pop three pills, hoping to get a blue-colored blur or some drowsy high that could make me laugh and get giddy, maybe let me defocus my vision. See places without centers or cornered ends. This will be my new meeting point in Grandma's apartment, a treasure box with morphine.

"You know that's not her real red hair."

"I didn't know," I say. I flush the toilet ostentatiously.

"I'm the one with the real red hair," Grandma tells me. "She stole my birthright."

The pills get stuck in my throat. I put my head under the faucet and turned on the cold water. I swallow two time-release pills.

"I thought she was the natural redhead," I say, coming out of the bathroom. "And you weren't."

"She's a liar."

"What difference does it make now?" I say.

"It makes her look old."

When I hear Grandma's pronouncements over redheads I remember my mother saying Grandma's hair color was made from auburn dye. I contemplate who are the real redheads.

I walk outside and sit on my grandma's front steps, to crack the first trip of the morphine. Grandma talks to me through the kitchen window while she is baking apple pies.

"Does she still have my diamond brooch?" Grandma asks. "That's mine too."

"It's in the vault."

"She stole my birthright," Grandma says.

"I have a check for you from my mother," I tell her.

"I don't want it," Grandma says. "She's owed me for years."

My eyes begin to unfocus as I turn sideways to stare up at Grandma's one-story Spanish stucco apartment, plaster falling off the sides. This building is designated a welfare compound. A chain-link fence has been put up all around the apartments and courtyard.

"Why won't you take the money?"

"I can take care of myself!" Grandma yells. "She thinks I'm some old lady who is an invalid." Grandma slams the window shut.

The small vegetable garden outside Grandma's steps of her apartment goes vertigo. Baby tomatoes growing out. My head becomes dizzy. The blood in my body moves slower. All I see is red, like the color of my red dreams as a child.

Ever since I was five years old, I've had dreams in red. I would wake up at 5 A.M. in a cold sweat and scream. My bedsheets would be soaking wet. I'd pull them from my bed and throw them on the floor. I would stare at the ceiling, my body cold and naked until morning.

Before I went to sleep I would leave all the lights on in my bedroom. The closet light was on and the closet door wide open so I could see the light. Every object in my bedroom had light on its surface. That way, nothing could become red at night.

I had my mother install deadbolts on my bedroom door. I owned a small gold key that locked my bedroom door behind me each night. I would sometimes put my ear to the door to listen if anyone was coming up the stairs.

Night after night when I was small, I listened to records that Grandma had given me, Puccini and Bellini arias. She told me Maria Callas was good for sleeping. La Divina could protect me from dreams.

Sometimes it became dawn and I hadn't fallen asleep. Soon my mother was giving me Nyquil so I could get drowsy and fall asleep to my Maria Callas records. I took ten spoonfuls of the green liquid. It tasted sour, and I knew it was laden with alcohol.

When I was thirteen, I went downstairs to my mother's liquor cabinet, under a Butsadon, which was formerly my grandmother's Buddhist altar. Grandma would have placed lily flowers in its blue ceramic offering bowl. The red apples would have sat on silver trays, beside white candles with purple orchids painted on their sides. Grandma would have placed before it a gold pillow with white fringe for kneeling and praying. My mother had taken the altar from her when Grandma lost it to my mother in a game of Mao. My mother used it for a liquor cabinet. The wood was a light brown. Under the curved roof was a bronze statue of Buddha wearing giant gold pearls draped across his body. The statue was missing an arm from when my mother's movers dropped it.

Inside the Gohonzon I found scotch. I poured it into little red teacups. My intake was five teacups a night.

Anyway, I had found a new way to fall asleep: Nyquil, one tenth of scotch, Maria Callas, and a Buddhist prayer.

Now I sit on Grandma's steps, my head buried between my legs. Then I walk back into the apartment, focusing enough to remove Grandma's combination padlock on her front door.

Inside Grandma's apartment is a Shangri-La. It has everything she has ever collected. Through my morphine gaze, objects are crisper and remain more permanent. There are many things in silver. Photo albums in black felt. Pictures of her on the slopes in Switzerland. Sitting in London cafés. Large dresses with stones on them, hanging on racks in the closet and falling to the floor amid moth-balls.

My posture tips as I walk down the one short hallway that leads from the living room to the kitchen. In the hall-way are more boxes and various mirrors: makeup mirrors, powder mirrors, a large round art deco mirror to go on a vanity, and a four-foot-square mirror. They all are lined on the floor against the walls with their backs facing out. They would make the apartment look bigger if they were hung, but Grandma is worried about flash reflections for photos.

Some are from the dressing rooms of her photo studios. The remaining ones are artifacts from Europe. Most of them come from my grandmother's house, which she lost to my mother in a game of Mao.

Grandma has covered all the windows with brown card-board. Each pane of glass is covered with square cutouts taped into place. She notices me notice them, as if I had never seen them before. "It's to avoid the bullets," she says, as she makes her apple pie for me. She is elegant as ever in this preserved space.

I place my hand in my pocket and pull out the long green check for Grandma. I walk toward her. "You can cash it at the bank."

"I don't want it."

"Why?"

"Don't ask stupid questions."

"My mother wants to help."

"I don't need her help."

I move closer to hand the check to Grandma, who backs off from me, pulling her arms behind her back. My hands attempt to meet her hand.

"Take it away." Grandma's voice begins to grow shrill. She sounds like my mother in a stage of panic. When they both go to this world of high girls' voices, I retreat.

I place the check near the twelve-inch black-and-white TV on the kitchen table in the corner, covered with dried apples, pears, and apricots in plastic bags.

"I'm not going to use it," Grandma declares. "She's wasting her checks."

Grandma is chopping up the sour green apples and dicing the raisins. It is a long process. It takes her all night. But I watch carefully, drugged, focused on the precision with which she lays the crust in slices to create the look of a glamorous pie. Everything she cooks has wheat and honey. I watch the way the honey falls from the spoon and sinks into the dough at 1 A.M.

Grandma stays all evening on her feet just as I imagine she did for so many years, walking the street looking for the right subject: an expressive face, a romantic moment, good lighting at dawn, an accident, or a force of nature to photograph. Now the cancer is killing her. I know it will take her. I watch the sliver of the knife as it cuts.

"I'm dying and I'm in love with it," Grandma says. She takes off her white rhinestone ring, shaped like a star, and kneads wheat and water for her second pie. Her tangerine-orange hair flashes under the kitchen lights. She collects citrus in this room. Lemons, grapefruits, and tangerines.

"How long does it take to bake?" I ask.

"What are you, the Pope? You want to pray over it or something?"

"No," I say. "Although I used to think you were God."

"What changed that?" Grandma asks.

"You got cancer."

Grandma reaches for her silver knife and begins to make cutout designs on the dough: a flower, a sun, and various geometric shapes.

"Even gods die," Grandma tells me. "Look at all the Greek myths."

"They didn't die of disease."

"You don't think they've got syphilis in heaven?"

"If they have sex," I respond. "Do you think they have sex in heaven?"

"Orgies."

"I don't know if I believe in heaven anymore," I tell her. "I'm not sure I believe in orgies either."

"Errol Flynn had them."

"When is the pie ready?" I ask. "What about a microwave?"

"It causes cancer."

"What does it matter now?"

"They don't tell us everything they know about radiation," Grandma says.

"Why can't we have a microwave?" I say to her, reaching unsteadily for a wedge of apple that fell to the counter. "Can't we just succumb to conformity? It would be easier to be like everyone. Everyone would like us," I say. "We could even act dumb." I sit on the stool watching Grandma roll out the pie, as if she were invisibly taking its picture.

"Your mother's on the run," Grandma says, intent on her work. "When your mother was thirteen we were on the run."

I work to focus on Grandma's fingers, bare and spotted with brown liver marks.

"I had to take her out of the hospital. They put her in there because they said she was schizophrenic."

I concentrate on my calves and thighs gripping the stool, as I feel a light tickling sensation from the pills, calming the vascular system down.

"It was the fifties," Grandma says. "They thought everybody was crazy." Grandma dices raisins. "She was at Camarillo."

I recede at the word Camarillo; it sounds like a city peopled with plagues. Is mental illness contagious? From what Grandma is saying, at Camarillo being sick is like being a witch, a heretic. They gave electric shock therapy to people who were moody, alien. Electric shock therapy takes away your memory, Grandma tells me. Sometimes I see my mother walking around with an empty head, drained of herself like milk from a carton.

I am able to listen to the story detached, my body and arms starting to relax on the stool. They could almost melt onto the wooden seat, sinking below to the ground.

"I worked day shifts and night shifts as a photographer and did four weddings in a day to pay the bills."

I regard my grandma's varicose veins, purple lines along her arms and legs, blood beating fast along the muscles and her vascular disorder; she got knotted veins from the work camps.

"Did you visit her?"

"On the weekends I would take her to the Santa Monica pier."

"What did you do?"

"She loved roller coasters. I was away a lot working," she adds.

"Doing what?"

"I was all over Europe as a photojournalist. The photo editors never thought I would go back to Germany, but I requested to work in Germany."

The fact that Grandma would go to Germany and want to be there suggests to me there is forgiveness.

"I sent pictures and chocolate to her at Camarillo," Grandma says. "She never wrote me back. I stopped writing her." She tosses apple cores into a side dish for scents she will one day make. "The doctors said she was violent. So they gave her electric shock therapy." Grandma tells me this in a sweet melodic voice, twice removed, telling somebody else's story. "She was twelve. They said she would get better. Nothing changed. She's still crazy."

Now Grandma's fists become clenched and work in a rote vertical line across the pie dough with a rolling pin. It clashes against the sharp ends of the kitchen counter, each time more labored and thrust forward. "They should have kept her in there longer." Then she breaks out into a shrill laugh. "I took her out one time for a weekend visit and never brought her back," Grandma says to me. "She's still registered there."

"Who was her father?" I ask. Maybe I'm not even interested, a brushed-aside curiosity.

"Why do you want to know so much?" Grandma gazes sternly at me. It's the first time she distrusts me, her voice edgy. " He died in a race car accident." Grandma looks away, concentrated on other objects, something that might be the truth. My mother tells me Grandma won't say who her real father is. I believe her race car accident is an elaborate legend, like the age differences and name changes on her passports and licenses. The identity of my mother's father is the one secret she cherishes.

In our family, we never inherit real last names. Grandma's last name was changed to escape France. Again, in Hollywood, she changed her pseudo last name because it didn't go well with her Hollywood logo, so her last name became Highland, "Highland of Hollywood." Tonight she is Ida Highland

She came to Hollywood to be Ida Highland after she saw it on a street sign. What did it matter? She has different names for each season. The last name on the gas bill is different from the last name on the telephone bill. I am unable to keep up perfectly with the scattered last names. So many names heaped together. Can you actually be that many people? Or are the names similar to costumes that you wear in a photo shoot or movie scene, when you wholly believe each role that you portray is nonfiction? Maybe the names are an elegy to the past, each last name worn for her seven dead brothers and sisters who died under the Third Reich.

I relinquished my last name to avoid identification with my father. So I took Grandma's fictitious surname.

The only name I owned was Jordan. That was real. My last name doesn't matter because it has been changed multiple times because of the Third Reich, bad credit, and escaping institutions. In this family we do not have time to reason for an identity. Our last names change as a means of escape.

"The state police were looking for us all across the West," Grandma says, her voice all pride. They traveled in a Studebaker station wagon along the coast of California, keeping my mother in warm wool blankets as they drove from motel to motel, changing IDs along the way. They got to Big Sur undetected, where they stayed in a white shack motel above the coast. Grandma listened for two weeks to my mother's stories from the hospital: The things the doctors did to little girls in private rooms—girls who were given lobotomies, the ones brought in for botched abortions, the ones who had electric shocks.

I imagine my mother's body restrained by her wrists tied to the metal bed posts, her face full of contempt as the nurses minister to her with anesthesia and muscle relaxants.

Mother told Grandma the voltage and the currents were like blue waves running through her temples and connecting to the brain. When she attempted to remember her life, everything came back as sounds without images.

"I promise you paradise," Grandma tells me she told my mother.

Grandma places the finished pie in the oven, which she closes with one bare foot. When she crouches down to stare into the oven window at the pie, she is avoiding my eyes. She's not looking to surrender her own composure, though she is on the verge of repentance and shame; she would not let me see her cry.

My thoughts are dissolving into an unknown high. And upon reflection I'm satisfied that my awareness level has fallen during Grandma's confessions. I prefer to be intoxicated when hearing the truth.

I move to the living room as Grandma finishes cleaning up. I am waiting to have my picture taken. Every weekend since I moved in, Grandma has photographed me. The living room is set up as a photo studio. Grandma's large format camera, the Hasselblad, sits on the tripod, connected by a wire to the umbrella flashes with silver tinfoil in the linings. The electrical cables are duct-taped to the corners of the room, and all lead to one giant generator that doubles as a coffee table. The whole apartment is pervaded with old Polaroid cameras, thirty-five millimeter cameras, burnt-out flashbulbs, light meters, batches of undeveloped black-and-white film stock in tiny black canisters, telescopic lenses, wide-angle lenses, tight lenses, boxes of wigs and costume jewelry for models, and large portable mirrors with light-bulbs.

A huge metal stand with rolls of paper is standing against the wall; it has different-colored backdrops in blue, yellow, and black. On the metal racks in one corner are the models' clothes that Grandma used for her pictures during the seventies: floor-length model dresses from Vegas, sequined gowns, hip huggers, orange knit miniskirts. Inside four tall boxes are fake eyelashes, old pancake makeup rotting in jars, assorted bikinis, bright fuchsia and green one-piece bathing suits, and shoes from the forties with corked high heels. Each box has different-colored wigs hanging out of the top, various flips in sienna and platinum blond. The wigs are dusty, the hair thin and pulled out from the nets.

Today, Grandma spent half of her $500 Social Security check to pay for all the food, film, and batteries.

Soon, I position myself in front of the lens as Grandma takes a Polaroid to test the composition and lighting. It takes three minutes for the chemicals to develop. Grandma shakes the Polaroid print ten times and checks her watch with such gravity she seems to be monitoring blood samples. In those three minutes of expectation, I count silently with Grandma. Then Grandma lifts the gray developing paper off the wet print. It smells of burning oil and has green liquids on the sides.

My feet patter around the apartment, watching with interest, Grandma's blue eye shadow on her eyes highlighted by the lights while she studies the print. When I see the print, I have a fallen smile, my pupils pinpointed from the morphine, and the lips overly red.

Grandma does not get dressed up for a shoot. She wears baggy blue jeans and soft running shoes that say LAS VEGAS in gold Roman lettering with a wreath. Grandma quickly pulls up her slightly sagging jeans. The cancer had already marked her; I could see the slow weight loss threatening her muscle.

"I'm finally getting my girlish figure back," Grandma says as she sees me register how her clothes hang on her. "I turn tragedy into glamour." Grandma strikes a pose of the pinup girl, her hands high above her head and legs thrust forward into a plié.

Then she violently shakes the Polaroid. She hands me a picture of Charlie Chaplin in *The Kid*. "I want you to look like Jackie Coogan in the movie." Grandma becomes a director at this point, orchestrating emotions and structuring the pose. She hands me a baseball cap. This was a part of the shoot she already had planned days before: the characters, mood, and setting.

Grandma tightly pulls the bill of the cap over to the side of my head so it is horizontal across my forehead. "You have to cheat," Grandma says.

"It's not natural," I say.

"This isn't about being real, it's about looking good."

"What's wrong with the way I look?"

"Your face is too round."

"My face isn't too round."

"You look better when you are in profile and then turn to the camera," Grandma says.

Does Grandma know I am high and refuses to admit it? I try to keep my eyes wide open, fighting against the weight of my eyelids.

I watched Grandma quickly adjust her tripod two feet higher. She uses a stepladder to climb up to view the camera. The camera is aiming at me from two feet up in the air.

"What's this for?"

"It's to make your face look more square."

"How?"

"The higher I am, the less the outline of your face becomes distinct."

I am off balance on the chair, and I do not question why everything in the room seems on an incline to the left.

"And smile," Grandma adds.

Taking pictures with Grandma and the movie I'm making when I live with Grandma use different mechanics of the brain. In films the camera shames me. With Grandma's camera I gain absolution.

When I become the object of anyone else's lens it begins with words like *disassociate editing, telescopic lens, aperture settings, light meters*. It all sounds like surgery to me. To be able to capture a moment in time on a strip of film almost takes away the spirit. I've read that certain tribes do not allow picture taking because it might steal the soul.

When the thirty-five millimeter movie lens is in front of my face, the reflection is the same from tinfoil, and I imagine heroin addicts when they try to chase the dragon. On top of the front of a camera, with its wide square face, are black sun protectors, leafs of metal on each side of the square that resemble butterflies in mourning.

When I stand in front of the movie lens I can't help feeling molested. I remember my father.

I remember what I forgot. In front of the camera I feel arms touching me in a type of sacred dance, and my father is constantly there.

I am posed in front of the camera, and I remember the enormity of the Pacific Ocean, curving its body along the coastline, and alongside some perpendicular reality of my father. I see his toes buried in sand except for his white crisp toenails, shaved at the ends with a thick white rim above the top.

As Grandma takes my picture, I see my father's face moving forward into me, beginning to take my clothes off, cradling me in his arms. I am watching it from the outside. My father and me, somewhere at the beach. Some white world, covered up. I've learned those sins are little indentations left around the body, that could be used in a close-up, but this torment would be too huge for the screen.

I can feel my father in me. Going inside and out, unable to stop, his knuckles on my skin, holding me by the nape of my neck, with me unable to see his mouth, and always resisting. My hand trying to hold onto the bedside cabinet, the half-filled glass tipping over. The drops on my hands from scotch, the little burns.

I was eight. I got up from my father's bed and walked into the kitchen, the dishes a stale odor piled in the sink, bones of chicken and rinds of fruit lying tattered all over the counters. I looked at my father's car keys on the counter, a silver glare. Could I drive away? Would my feet reach the gas? How far could I go?

I walked over to my father's red shorts, feeling inside the sandy pockets, taking out two twenty-dollar crinkled bills damp from the ocean and coins that I grasped tight in my palms. I thought of train rides through the West, small engine aircrafts over the Congo. Where could the forty dollars take me?

I left the house, walking down the pavement with my clothes in my hand. I was trying to make for the end of the driveway, stepping over the sage, over rocks collected along my father's porch in magenta, lavender, and bronze, colored and aged by the sun.

I stood on Pacific Coast Highway, my shirt off, in my underpants, trying to look for a place to hide. My feet blistered on the hot asphalt in June. I did not know which way was north or south, back home to my mother's house or my grandmother's apartment. I got dressed and went to the gas station and got change from my father's bills and spent ten dollars at the vending machine buying chocolate bars, fruit jellies, and butter cookies.

I hid in some bushes when I saw my father's silver Porsche move slowly along the highway looking for me. I waited in the bushes until night fell, eating the square Danish butter cookies and chocolate bars. Later I heard my mother screaming out my name, frantically searching the road with her headlights, her head outside the window of her aged Mercedes. I listened for an hour to my mother yelling out Jordan Highland! Jordan Highland! I contemplated the idea of disappearing, walking along the highway and getting stolen. I wiped the blood away along my insides and groin with leaves, hoping not to be detected. I came out of the bushes after an hour and walked up to my mother, who held her high heels in her palms, walking barefoot along the highway.

"It's just a game," I told her.

Now, when I stare into Grandma's lens, I see the brown prism of light in her eyes. It is warm and serene, a soft wet space that I am insulated into.

Grandma changes a lens as I recall my father. Tonight in Grandma's apartment, Los Angeles is a fragmented memory, a distant paradise, and October becomes another broken Fahrenheit record.

"You're not smiling," Grandma tells me. "You've got to smile."

18

At five that morning I waited outside for Grace to leave the Deja Vu.

"Where are you going?" I ask.

"To go make some cash."

I follow her down Hollywood Boulevard at dawn. "I don't want you to do this," I say.

"You want to get high?" she asks.

"Yes."

"Then watch how I earn it," Grace tells me. "A quick drive around the block."

"There are other ways."

"You have any ideas?"

"I get a check by Friday," I say.

Grace stares at me blankly.

"I could get it from my mom."

"Where is she?"

"She'll be out of town for a few more days."

"What happens when the stuff runs out?" she says. "What happens when there's nothing left to come down with. Then what?"

"We'll go straight."

"In order to go straight we need something to come

down with," Grace tells me. "I'm not doing a nosedive."

"What's that?"

"When you come off with nothing. Not even any down-
ers. Not even a Vicoden," Grace says. "It's like diving into a
pool and landing on your stomach."

19

Every weekend I get high from Grace's junk.

On Saturday night in Grandma's apartment, there is only an aperitif of momentary lost time. No clocks, nothing ticking. It's a dead silence. I can hear only softness, the silk shirt being removed, and arms reaching out from under the falling cuffs. I can see her bare back silhouetted slightly from behind the silk screen with Mount Fuji painted in gold leaf along the partition. Her flesh is sticking out, small bones of the shoulder blades. They are smaller than mine.

Tonight there is the smell of stale milk in Grandma's apartment, or aged mozzarella.

Grandma has an innate ability to detect a personality by smells. A person has many many layers, she told me, and together they might mean something. The first smell, she said, was misleading, but if you stayed around the person long enough, you would pick up new scents: a drink, dinner, last bedroom, job. Most smells were decoders. When she was searching for models, she acted like a cowboy, checking the turf vigilantly. She would talk to one guy and dismiss him by the scent. "I don't like his smell, it's old, and something's wrong with him," she would say.

Grandma's texture is of oil and bronze, very fragrant and pure. And when I'm near her I can smell the whispering on the wheat as the wind blows over the stalks, brushing them together back and forth.

In front of me is the smell of burning tobacco, the damp rolled paper, and saliva along the tips of Grandma's mouth. The white thin smoke rising into my nostrils. It's what I imagine mercury to smell like, or silver. It's cold and tasteless. The dead ashes in the ashtray remind me of old hotel rooms, the hotel apartments on Figueroa and Broadway in downtown Los Angeles, where I can buy speed.

Grandma takes this room hostage. Old paisley-patterned gray wall paper, blotched with yellow water stains. The smell of corroded metal on the bedsprings of the pull-out bed in the apartment. With green wool blankets. And a striped pillowcase that is dense with cotton but has gotten stiff and does not bend. A dark lime wall, the paint so thick I can still see where wet paint spots dried. A six-inch black-and-white television set with rabbit ears held together by tinfoil, crunched and looking like the tinfoil that holds heroin. The TV's volume is turned down, the screen a strobe light across the walls.

Grandma and I have something in common, I realize: our tainted bodies. Her back, slightly bent, disjointed and bruised, reminds me of when she was a German officers' girl in France, making bargains with her body to save her family during the Second World War. The German men took her up to their houses in the Sixth Arrondissement, and they had her wear red patent leather shoes, the stiletto heels at five inches.

From behind the screen Grandma is telling me how the German officers liked orgies, how they passed her around like in Japanese tea ceremonies. Each leg offered to the next man on the left, then the leg passed on to the left, clockwise.

Grandma goes over to the armoire. She opens up the drawers filled with the black-and-white snapshots in plastic bags.

"They gave me silver and gold for gifts," Grandma says. "Then I sold them and got the money." With her left hand, Grandma throws a stack of old snapshots on the floor. "I took their pictures," she says. "It helps me to not forget."

I reach for the stack of pictures, five by six and black around the sides, pieces of flesh in the centers. They remind me of mug shots or scenes from serial killings. I touch the rims of the photographs.

Grandma sits down in front of me, her silk kimono opened down the center, her legs crossed. She is wearing white house slippers made out of quail feathers.

"Grace?" Grandma asks.

"I think we'll break up."

"What does that mean?"

It's always about the next fix, I want to tell Grandma. Grace is always on the hunt for it. She and I will die if we continue.

And I think about my body. How I'm an insect or some floating ego. I was never aware of my own body, it was something I carried around. It was like a box that had a voice and no face and was figureless. It was like I was part of some space and I floated within the circumference of it, occasionally letting my hands touch the surface. I wondered if it had something to do with my father, his ignoring. It has a type of vanishing effect on someone, that people can make you disappear.

I compare my body reflected against Grandma. When I look at Grandma, I start to see my own body, I see what she sees. Purple blotches under my eyelids, the smooth and deep indentures, like rotting ivory. In the dark red chair I sit in, I see my backbone is curving and hardly offering support. If I put my hands through my hair, it will be stiff and oily. My arms are bruised down their centers, small scabs covering up past entrances. Now I only shoot up through the rectum because I don't want Grandma to identify my habit.

Grandma brings tea, the steam covering her face from mine. The psychedelic printed butterflies on her robe seem to be flying through the steep of the tea.

A few moments later, inside the bathroom, I have my head deep in the bowl, the drain flushing water in my ears, as I throw up the various pills. And the cold water plumbing makes everything all right. Grandma walks up from behind me and holds me in the middle of the butterflies.

I sit in her arms, trying to imagine what type of liquids they are putting in her. If we could only live in Paris. What does the Seine look like from a hospital bed? She would be restrained, the knots around her wrists, holding onto the side bars, holding on and maybe trying to catch a breath from the Seine.

It was during the German occupation in France that she left; the glass bottles on the vanity survived the trip. A combination of pungent scents still whirled around me whenever I walked into her apartment.

I hoped one day I could find her a better place to die in. I would have liked to take her on a cruise across the Atlantic and let her see Paris again.

"I'm going to move to the desert, get a camper," she said as we looked at Matisse's *Lady in the Blue Dress*. Her painted red nails were beautiful. Grandma was always talking of escape.

20

For the next week I shoot up speed with Grace every morning at six o'clock to get through the past two weeks of shooting, but on Sunday of the second week my mother and Grandma are playing Mao at the Farmers Market.

"You've got to go back to the doctor," my mother says. "The X rays show it could spread into the blood. You have to take some therapy."

Grandma does not look at my mother. "Leave me alone."

"Do this for us," Mother says.

"Pass the next card."

"Do you want to die?" Mother asks.

"I don't want to talk about it.'"

"What if I win the game?"

"Two games out of four," Grandma says, her hands shuffling the cards, "and I'll go to a doctor."

An hour later, at dusk, the vendors begin the long ritual of closing their *bodegas*. And Grandma wins four games out of four.

21

Every night Grandma develops pictures. Five by seven, eight by ten, and even thirty-five millimeter negatives.

This takes five hours. No one can use the bathroom for five hours. "Pee in the bushes," Grandma tells me.

The negatives have different photographers' names on the folders, not Grandma's. They match some of the names on phone and electric bill notices around the apartment.

"Why do you have so many names?" I ask Grandma.

"It all depends," Grandma says. "One for each season."

"Can you actually be that many people?"

In the bathroom is a faint red light. I watch her develop negatives she has found.

After she reviews all the contact sheets, Grandma begins printing. The light projects the negative on paper. Then Grandma places her hands with the print in the developing fluid. These liquids sting and make scabs. Some people wear face masks; Grandma wanted to breathe in the picture.

In the past three weeks I have learned the code words of the darkroom. The prints sit under D–1 and stop bath for twenty minutes. The timer is set. Grandma listens to Chet Baker when she prints.

Grandma is printing pictures she had taken of my mother. They were taken in the fifties. This is a chance for Grandma and my mother to be together—and now, on the developing prints, they collide once again.

"Why are you so angry at my mom?"

"She doesn't know how to play Mao," Grandma says. "Once she threw a glass vase at my head. I had fourteen stitches."

She places the eight-by-ten prints under running water in the bathtub for twenty minutes to wash off the chemicals.

"What are you looking for in the pictures?" I ask Grandma.

"My daughter."

"Why do you have to find her in a picture? She lives only ten minutes away."

"In the pictures, I think she's saying 'I love you.'"

"I think in the pictures she is also saying 'Call me.'"

Later, Grandma finally begins hanging the prints on laundry lines.

We sit for hours, waiting for the images to dry. The eight-by-ten prints are held by clothespins, dripping wet from chemicals. These are Grandma's forms of forgiveness. Printing what she remembers. Printing what she wants to see.

22

"Van Gogh was in love with Gauguin." Grandma is braiding her hair. "That's why he cut off his ear." She combs the knots out of the ends, then joins three strands together.

A few days later, Grandma and I are again talking in her bathroom. I wait to be picked up by my mother for an awards ceremony.

"Why did he kill himself?" I ask.

"He couldn't paint anymore."

I see what Van Gogh felt in the little room in the South of France, how he would stare at the mirror for hours, contemplating his death, analyzing his skin tones and the movements of bone structure.

"Van Gogh would crack the mirror and stare at himself through the broken glass," she says.

"Are you going to die?" I ask.

"Photographers never die, they just fade away like an old print," Grandma tells me.

"I don't believe in heaven," I say.

"Heaven can be a gigantic camera."

Then Mother was banging on the front door, and the whole apartment shook.

"Don't let her in," Grandma says. She walks into the living room and turns on Mozart at one hundred decibels. It's no. 41, *Jupiter*. "She's bad luck," Grandma says.

"Meet me here tonight," she tells me over the music.

Grandma scrambles around the house, blocking the windows with more cardboard.

"Where are we going?"

"Laughlin."

Grandma pulls down all the shades in the apartment. "Don't tell your mother where we're going."

I walk out of Grandma's apartment and stare at the screens on the windows, blackened from dirt. Through the opening of the door, I can see that the red satin lamp with fringes is on, like the fabric on flappers' dresses in the twenties. The chair under the lamp is empty. And the whole horizon of where the chair sits seems about fifty yards away.

Those moments watching Grandma die, it's like Weegee, who was there to take the picture almost before the crime happened. In black and white, the blood looked like chocolate. What Weegee could do was silently step under the yellow ribbons marked DO NOT CROSS, and be present for the crime's aftermath, the victim's last breath. He gave life to the almost-dead gangster on the curb, the .22 in the puddle, and the maroon holes. Or the husband who stuck the meat cleaver into his wife's back. Weegee did not take out the blade in her back. He lit the flashbulb, printed the picture, and saved her murder.

I take Grandma's death and put it under halogen lamps. Surface the picture with Vaseline, apply it to the lens of the camera. Lay the body out on the floor, test the light, and save her.

In the darkroom, I would do the retouching and stitch in photos of Paris, my mother, my father, and myself. Place the picture under the developing light and superimpose other images across the picture. Burn in the picture at the sides: leave the light on for five minutes. The white in the picture will be gone, the print will get darker, and I will see cancer.

23

The next morning, Grandma and I pack for Laughlin, Nevada. Grandma opens a metal box filled with rubies and diamond brooches. I figure she must have gone to the bank, to some security box. Grandma is bringing her jewelry in case we need more money to gamble, or for gas.

She dumps her orange pill bottles and painkillers for the road into the suitcase. Grandma is also bringing her camera equipment and lighting stands. She is planning on taking pictures of the desert and me.

I also plan to carry her boxes of negatives, all five of them. She intends to organize all her original negatives while we camp in the desert.

"Someone stole my original negatives," Grandma says, her voice violent. "Did your mother come in here?" she asks.

"I'm not my mother's keeper."

Grandma finishes packing her suitcase. She throws in a long silver-and-black sequined gown and a green-dyed fur coat. "I bet she stole them," Grandma says, closing the valise. "She's a thief."

"Why would she?"

"She wants to get her hands on everything before I die."

Today I know the real reason why Grandma is paranoid. Grandma is going out to the desert to find a doctor who smuggles in illegal medicine for cancer. And she doesn't want to get caught.

"It's us against them now," Grandma says.

While Grandma and I drive through the desert, I'm at the steering wheel, even though I'm fifteen and don't have a learner's permit.

"What about cops?" I ask.

"It's Nevada!" Grandma says.

I see a desert sun at high noon on the way to Laughlin, Nevada. The empty roads and arid land patches give me the feeling we're arriving at some last depository, traveling through rain-shadowed deserts that only received water on windward mountains.

Grandma has sprayed herself with jasmine and roses, the whole Winnebago intoxicated with her scents.

"I'm searching for light," Grandma tells me. "I need the right light." Grandma reclines into the passenger seat, not resigned, her neck still straight and poised. Grandma has said this is the last sitting in the desert she will be photographing. It will end the collection.

"We don't say our names; we don't tell them anything," Grandma says. She was counting crisp hundred-dollar bills with her fingers, licking the sides and rolling them up in tinfoil. "We get the stuff and leave."

She stuffs the white envelope with cash into the glove compartment and locks it. Her gold ring glimmers, its one pearl glaring against mirrors and sun, the gold band warm and burning around her ring finger. Her arms are hanging out of her low-cut summer dress, a white slip underneath the transparent silk.

"Five hundred dollars for a couple more months,"

Grandma says. "It's a rip-off." I wonder if we could get enough money to buy twenty years. Grandma has her neck sticking out the car window, the hot breeze blowing across her profile and through her dress, ruffling the lily print. In the wind, her skin becomes wrinkleless.

"He lives in some shack. He breeds rattlesnakes, he uses their venom for the stuff. " She pauses and reaches into her purse and pulls out a bag of spliff. "It's good for my health," she tells me, as if I asked.

"That's my pot," I say.

"We'll share." Grandma takes out the bag and rolling paper and begins picking out the seeds along her lap in between her painted red nails, her cut cuticles perfectly shaped with crescent-mooned heads.

"Do you have a driver's license, Grandma?"

"I didn't pass the eye test." Grandma passes me the wet end tip of grass. I inhale the joint and pass it back to Grandma.

Watching the desert, I'm on another planet. I think about how much the French love deserts. It's probably the lack of humidity. The desert is hallucinogenic. Just witnessing so many forms of cacti is like learning a new language. Cactus in burnt oranges struggling to survive. The San Jacinto Mountains we drive through, Diamond Mountains, Humboldt River Mountains, and Shoshone Mountains rise next to Indian burial grounds, and I know there is voodoo in this landscape. Huts with old broken-down cars on mountaintops with electrical windmills. I think they transmit something.

Grandma's smoke hazes the whole view inside the Winnebago, and I breathe in every last chance of green pleasure. Grandma tips the ashes of the rolled paper gently, as if putting out a pipe in an opium den in Paris. There she would be content with the last puff of Turkish opium, lay down the gold flute, and later have a small glass of bitter absinthe on a table within arm's reach to alleviate the hot blaze, the anise giving a boost to the brown-yellowish smoke in her lungs.

"We need to find a dumpy motel," Grandma says, from her deep reclining seat and desert high.

24

Grandma is throwing up the venom in the bathroom of the Geronimo Motel.

Grandma walks out of the bathroom, a towel covering her mouth, wiping away the traces of venom on the corners of her lips. "I'm throwing up snakes," Grandma says.

In the motel we sequester ourselves from the cops. We pull down the shades, push the TV set and console as a barricade for the front door. I disconnect the phone. Grandma and I become one. We rehearse our pleas for insanity. We travel like criminals.

Grandma passes out on the bed. This is the first time I have ever seen Grandma get weak.

While Grandma sleeps, I ponder if Grandma dreams in black and white. The red badges of the Third Reich. The falcon on the flag. The capillaries in the eyes of the S.S. officers. She would have photographed these images with her small and soundless Leica camera, dependable enough for wars, with Kodachrome transparency that was rich in tone and sharpened out the lines. Like Margaret Bourke-White, Grandma carried a electronic flash that could dispel shadows and make bright silvered spots all over her landscape, expose the plight of glamour.

Maybe Grandma dreams about the fifties and the night-club in the Riviera Hotel in Las Vegas, where they took your picture at the table. I have seen a picture like that. It's black and white, and Mother is wearing a black cotton dress with a tiny pendant in the shape of an arrow, her hair pulled back into a bun. I don't know how old she was in the picture. Maybe sixteen. She was the temptation of cameras. With her petite body and small feet and hands, she was able to fit into the lens. Grandma shows her off to all the star makers like a miniature statue. Grandma told her to wear her hair back because it showed her features: the pointed nose, the wide brown eyes, the wide forehead. She bore the look of a very young Grace Kelly but with auburn hair. Grandma taught her how to sit down at a table, to move in casually like a wave, keeping the back straight and chin up, fall in to the dinner table in slow motion, eyes wide open and trying not to blink. Grandma told my mother to avoid creasing her forehead where lines began to show, to laugh gently so there would be no creases under her eyes. "I had to look like a river current," my mother has told me.

Maybe the photo taken was the night Marlene Dietrich was performing at the Sahara Hotel. Marlene was wearing a transparent gown with silver beads and a white fur that had a train, champagne breath, under a pink light, singing "La Vie en Rose."

After dinner, Grandma and my mother went backstage at the shows with Marlene Dietrich, Jayne Mansfield, Donald O'Connor, and the showgirls. I know my mother's first glimpse of backstage scenery inspired her to offer her soul for the monumental amounts of yellow dyed quail feathers and bright dressing-room bulb fixtures, the thick round pearl necklaces and gold-beaded bustiers, and the bright sheen of silk stockings. Mother stood behind the camera lens watching Grandma position the showgirl model wearing pedal pushers rolled up beyond the knees, adjusting the length of her hair, clipping the model's angora sweater in the back with clothespins to accentuate the points of the bra, almost making the wire-rimmed bra visible through the burgundy sweater. Mother was studying each move and detail, preparing for her chance in front of the camera.

My grandmother and my mother traveled to Las Vegas since my mother was a child in the fifties. Grandma had her camera equipment stored in the backseat up to the roof, blocking out all rear views for the two hundred miles from Los Angeles, the barren road leading to showgirls on the dunes and men in Brooks Brothers black suits, thin black ties, and horn-rimmed sunglasses. Grandma and my mother would be chased out of the sea desert by the black suits because Grandma's camera was too conspicuous.

My mother and I have both experienced Grandma's escape to the desert. We are both Grandma's children. These drives to the desert are a passage, a way for Grandma to expose us to the camera, her history, and time travel, a last oasis.

Grandma has brought thirty of her sketchbooks to the desert. The rest were in her closet at home. The sketches are in brown and charcoal, of people's bodies. Grandma sketched a lot of her subjects before she took the picture.

She knows the dimensions of physiognomy. But she was looking for the physical gestures of a subject that mirrored the interior soul: a hand held over the forehead or limbs exhausted over the couch, even the muscles along the arms in the right light.

With her Rolleiflex, skin becomes like bronze in black-and-white. The skin tones in her photos are opiates. She took pictures of pinups in Kodacolor. She was the first woman to do so. The photographs were used to boost the morale of soldiers. Retouching was her favorite part. Hiding the birthmarks. Covering up lost sleep, bloodshot eyes, cracked noses, baby fat, wrinkles, unwaxed arms, and deep circles under the eyes.

That's before she got into candids and Polaroid black-and-whites. The stars had to trust you; otherwise you didn't get a photo. She knew how to open them up like a seed.

She photographs to show herself as well. "If you stare long enough at the print, you can see the autobiography of the photographer," Grandma used to tell me.

I sit in the bed and imagine this is where Edward Hopper might have stayed. He and his wife, Jo. Scattered on the floor are wet white towels, pages of dialogue I had to memorize for the movie; we had tightly packed unopened suitcases, cold sheets, cars abandoned outside our room, and the four dark maroon walls that separate us from the highway that takes Grandma and me deeper into Nevada. I cannot sleep. The pink neon sign, GERONIMO MOTEL, is right above the room. Geronimo is wearing spurs and a cowboy hat and is staring west.

In Edward Hopper's painting *Western Motel*, Hopper's wife was the subject, an abandoned Mary, her light stolen from Vermeer, in a burgundy dress falling slightly below the knees. Watching Hopper in the painting, she is making a prayer for one last acknowledgment, knowing he will abandon her again for a landscape.

All I see outside the window is a highway leading out of the Geronimo Motel, out of Nevada out of these last-ditch efforts.

25

A few hours later the dreams began.

In my dreams I am at the ocean with my father.

I carried my backpack to the marina, filled with blank notebooks, math books, clothes my mother folded for me with my name printed on a tag and ironed onto the waistbands of my underwear and the collars of my shirts, pieces of scrap paper with numbers in case of an emergency, scrawled in my mother's handwriting in giant blue-ink letters, barely legible. I sometimes thought if she had written them better, more clearly, all that happened would have been prevented.

Sometimes I watched the sun rise through the skylight on my father's boat. We would be sailing along the Malibu coastline. The coast was jet black. Inside the boat I felt a cold draft off the morning waters.

I was on the bottom deck, on the bed, snuggled tightly into the corner. The skylight was open. I saw the blue sky get ready for sun. A cool breeze slipped through the opening.

My body was tired, the joints weakened by the late hour of dawn, my eyes half fixed on the day, drowsy and making out images of my father cooking on the stove, removing blankets, and passing me pillows on the bed. I was weakened by my father's frequent surge of energy in the bottom deck, searching for some object he would use, going in drawers, opening boxes.

As we sailed away I imagined my mother at the shore, having just missed us leaving, her face growing fainter as the boat left port, her arms reaching, unable to capture the ocean distancing me from her. My mother could not swim. She had a phobia of the deep end in a pool.

Later, my legs hung tied up in the air against two steel beams above the bed. My knees were held tightly against the iron posts.

The razor was like a cool breeze on my body. Gently it clipped the fibers of my hair out of their roots. The shave took a half hour. His head bobbed as he made the razor cuts along my center. Each time, the blade cut closer, making a swift cut around the entrance to my body.

"You look clean," Father told me.

The boat rocked left and right. The Pacific Ocean was under my back, moving with a mild tide. The boat tipped to the right, waiting to dump me into the ocean. I could have floated to Japan.

26

"We're running out of money," Grandma says a few days later as we check out of the Geronimo Motel.

"What about the jewelry?" I ask.

"I don't want to sell it." Grandma opens the door of the Winnebago and I get inside.

We drive west. This is not a savanna but dry cracked clay, reaching all the way past Death Valley, Barstow, Riverside, Montclair, and into Los Angeles.

A few hours later we are hungry. We decide to go to a coffee-shop diner. Grandma and I change in the camper in the parking lot, the headlights off and the Winnebago a dark place on the flat road between Nevada and the eastern entrance on our way back into California. We pretend it's Paris.

We are ten miles west of Laughlin. Behind us in the middle of pitch-black desert terrain are phosphorescent lights barely discernible in the dense air, various motels in psyche-delic neon colors, and casinos. Their signs stand out like waving hands in the middle of the discontented desert: pictures of aquamarine pools alongside wilted palms on the highway, casinos with money signs posted in glittering silver sequins, windblown with the last hot gasp of day and shining off the moon.

"Let's go to the Moulin Rouge," Grandma says as she dresses in the bathroom. She is going to wear a long black-lace dress that has a slit down the middle of the bodice.

I stand behind her in the bathroom rolling layers of her skin tightly into the skintight dress and lifting the zipper of her dress solidly along the spine. Grandma's body fits snugly into the fabric, which stretches with her aged body. She tells me she had the smallest waistline in Paris. Even now she still is smaller than most women. Grandma reaches around the shape of her body, checking its directions, preening out the creases and altering the dress to her shape with thin tugs of her fingers.

"I wore this dress with a prince. He would have left the throne for me." Grandma starts to place jewels on her hand. "I could have married anyone."

Grandma puts on her red ruby ring, the size of a bottle cap, inlaid in platinum. It's unbreakable and transparent all the way down to the pink skin on Grandma's finger.

I'm wearing a black velvet tuxedo suit and shiny black patent-leather shoes, tight along my toes, and the tuxedo tie splitting at the ends, unable to make a clean circle around my neck. I wore this tuxedo to my father's inauguration into the Football Hall of Fame when I was ten. I had gotten dressed out of fear, with the detachable black and silver buttons, the clip-on black satin tie, loose cuff links. They were all accessories to look happy. My mother kept combing my hair forward, gel and hairspray, adjusting the cuffs and shoulders of the jacket methodically, wanting me to look presentable to my father.

I sat in the audience, my palms cobbled tight around the arms of the chair. The ginger ale I had drunk went through me, my body felt cold and dejected, and I was unable to smile. I had sat in the car with my father and mother on the way to the presentation; it was the only time we traveled together.

It was soundless inside the car, the doors locked, the windows tinted. Our shoulders and chests were squeezed together on the car seats. We had to look at each other. We had to be a family because of space. I sat in the car and pretended my mother would be wearing a wedding ring from my father, he would hold her arms in his hands, and I would be a real son. I would be in the Boy Scouts, and my father would be a scout leader, or I could play football with my father, the team coach.

I was wearing white socks, and they caught my father's attention. He told me I couldn't wear white socks, and then he took off his black socks and gave them to me, slipping his bare feet back into his maroon penny loafers. The removal of the socks and him wearing no socks in the shoes reminded me of how he liked to strip. He always wanted to wear as little as possible. I knew my father did not wear underwear with his jeans or slacks. I had seen them come off quickly before, revealing his bared torso and hips. And I would turn away as the body walked in my direction, making me into something naked too.

Most of the time he did not wear socks with hard leather shoes. I put on the black socks in that car, feeling his post-game sweat trailing up the base of my foot and ankle, his fifty-yard calluses brittle suggestions to my bare feet. He said the socks would be good luck.

In the camper, the suit is splitting at the seams, tight along my chest and rib cage; I am not able to connect the buttons with the holes. My hair is slicked back with Brilliantine gel, and my skin is soft and pink. Grandma has me wash my face with a warm wet rag and has me keep my face in a hot steam towel for ten minutes as I breathe through it. She says the treatment will make me look like a movie star afterward. Meanwhile, as the towel consumes me, Grandma has cucumbers on her eyes and avocados spread across her skin. Her hair is up in black wire-rimmed curlers. She says I look dark and Spanish.

I go along with it. I look ridiculous, although I feel like Philip V of Spain with Grandma. She has a way of making people feel important. She takes her left arm and slides it into my grip as we walk the three steps across the camper to the mirror. We could be on our way to the opera with our own private booth and our own sets of ivory opera glasses.

"I could have been a duchess." Grandma is applying red lipstick on her lips, pouring herself into the mirror. The lipsticks are old and chapped at the heads; Grandma uses a small thin paintbrush to dig out the remaining color. The foundation bottles are thick and crusted with age. When Grandma applies the wet grease, her whole face changes into a bronze. With a thick brush, she dusts rose blush along her neckline and cheeks and above the cleft in her chest.

"I know you are the most beautiful woman in Paris," I tell her.

"They also always said I had the best profile in Paris."

Grandma is dressed and ready for the Moulin Rouge. "Did you make reservations?" she asks, as she grabs her mink stole, though it's Indian summer in the desert.

As we walk to Denny's, Grandma turns her rings under her hands to hide her jewels. She turns the green-dyed fur coat inside out, revealing a lining of green and white silk stripes.

"Don't you know who I am?" Grandma asks the waitress inside Denny's. She always has a way of defining herself to the head of a restaurant.

We get what we decide is the best table. Grandma never

gives up. We know there is going to be a show that night. Grandma likes big shows, from the Earl Carroll Girls to the Folies-Bergère.

Grandma has brought an old *Screen World* magazine with her. "I loved *Mildred Pierce*." She takes out a pair of scissors from her purse. "I took that picture. They stole it from me." Grandma starts to cut out the picture from the magazine. "Let's get a steak," she says.

"I'm a vegetarian."

"Meat's good for you," Grandma insists. I sit staring at Joan Crawford's face on the cover of the magazine. I start to have visions that she could be sitting at the next table.

"Don't listen to your mother," Grandma says. "She's anemic."

Later, I am terrified when the waitress brings the steak over.

"Eat it, you need the iron." Grandma cuts the meat into squares and starts to chew it ferociously.

I was told Grandma's cancer was enormous. I just sit and don't say anything. I wonder how big it is. Does it look like a football? Does it spread like a lake and go on forever? Could she get claustrophobic in her own body?

"Maybe you should go to a doctor," I say.

"They're all murderers, those doctors." Grandma is still chewing.

"Doesn't it hurt?" I ask.

"I don't know what you're talking about." Grandma stares at my overfilled plate. "Eat your steak."

"The tumors," I say.

"Leave me alone," Grandma says, as she shifts positions in the restaurant. "I'll be fine."

"I know it's giving you pain."

"I get a little uncomfortable," Grandma says. Her face looks the other way.

"Can you at least see a doctor?"

"They can't do anything," Grandma tells me.

"What about doing it for me?" I ask.

"Maybe."

"Do you promise?"

"We'll see," Grandma tells me.

All through dinner, I listen to the crashing of coins coming out of slot machines. I start to get restless. I can smell the boxes of negatives from the camper, even in the restaurant. I know they are feeding Grandma's brain. I can smell the chemicals and the rotting of film when I open the latches.

"Let's get out of here. They have no style," Grandma says, pushing the plate of steak away from her. "The meat's too tough."

"Maybe we could dance at the karaoke bar," I suggest.

"Let's do the tango!" Grandma says.

"I can learn anything fast," I tell Grandma. I had taken ballet lessons for three years, starting when I was seven, and believed that a dancer can do any dance because he understands the language of rhythm and surrender. When I dance I allow myself the trust that I could lead, take the leap with the change in beats, and hold up my partner.

"I used to dance in the Earl Carroll Girls revue," Grandma says, wiping the bloody steak juice off her hands with a napkin, then opening a shining black-glass compact and checking the rear of the room out of the mirror.

"What haven't you done?" I ask Grandma.

"I haven't been back to Paris," Grandma tells me. "The only way to understand Paris is by arriving there by ship."

I could hear the band next door, a trumpet, a reed, bass sax, congas; it was a quintet playing Cubana Bop, "A Night in Tunisia."

"Coming into port in the dense green-fogged waters and the torches of light at the harbor, then taking the train from

Le Havre at night across France," Grandma says.

"Let's go," I say. "I'll get the money."

"We'll go in December. After I get my negatives in order," Grandma says. "I have to leave the negatives in order for you."

"You're not going to die," I tell Grandma. "Don't even think that way."

"Let's dance." Grandma gets up from the table and sticks out her arms, her wrists limp, waiting in the air for me to bow and ask for her company, be the gentleman caller.

Grandma and I begin to dance in the middle aisle of Denny's restaurant to the loud bop music.

"Isn't this chic?"

After one song in Denny's I escort her next door to the dance floor. We walk in and there is no bop band, only a karaoke bar stocked with silver slot machines.

A man with one leg is lip-synching to a Frank Sinatra cover, "Chicago."

Grandma and I do our own combination of swing, waltz, and the intangible passion of the tango. Grandma holds me and we move to a fast one-two.

We are on the ground floor of La Coupole restaurant in Montparnasse. This karaoke bar is our La Coupole, where older women came to pick up young men on Sundays in the twenties.

Grandma is light as air. She spins me around in all directions. I hold on to her hands tightly. I take the dance very seriously. We stare into each other's eyes and dissolve rhythmically from step to step. The bop music dictates our beat, and we let our feet become slow, slow, fast, fast.

Our dance is more like the tango, where everything is surrendered. I give myself to Grandma. It's the safest embrace in the world.

*   *   *

At 4 A.M. we walk back to the camper, our bodies filled with inexorable heat made from dancing, our numb toes crushed against the soles of our shoes. Grandma's toes in her velvet-heeled shoes with brass tips, I imagine, are purple and bruised.

I fall into the bed with my clothes on and realize in two days we will go back home. I cradle the pillows; knees and hands lock deep into the feathers.

Grandma walks over to me in the dark, her rhinestone earrings shining from the moonscape outside. The slow movement of her silk dress overlaps on my bed. She pulls a book out. It's *Tropic of Cancer* by Henry Miller.

"Don't tell your mother. She doesn't understand. This was banned. That's what you need."

She places the book at the corner of my bed. And she walks away toward the bathroom to remove her second face.

I open the red-bound book, dust on the leaves of the pages, the paper thin and yellowed with age. The pages would break if I turned them too suddenly. On the front page is a quote from Emerson. "These novels will give way, by and by, to diaries or autobiographies—captivating books, if only a man knew how to choose among what he calls his experiences that which is really his experience, and how to record truth truly."

A shaft of white light shapes in the corner, and I can hear water running in the bathroom, the gallon it takes to remove Grandma's thick greasepaint.

I look through the camper's window and stare out at the desert, a desolate midnight on the dunes with fragments of scarlet neon light flickering, being turned off, the whole sky a baby-blue night with the spotlights and rainbow sensibilities of Nevada.

27

The next morning in the desert the sky is our backdrop, a giant square, full blue at all rims, gracing the rugged Sierra Nevada Mountains, the fallen bedrock on the roads a blue gelatin print in a composite including the desert.

Grandma is searching for eternity.

She sits on her beach chair at the edge of the camper, smoking pot. She is getting a suntan. She has on goggles to protect her eyes and a one-piece black nylon bathing suit. Mozart is blaring across the desert from the camper.

Grandma smokes cautiously, and when she exhales she does it slowly, the way a duchess would smoke at a mirthful dinner party. I think of women with braided hair bonnets in lace dresses and high collars flanking the men with fire and lighting their cigars. The candelabras lit and oil in the lamps, the men of letters with quail ink-stained fingers. These were the baroque sentiments that Grandma inspired.

"Listen to that finale." Grandma sways her arms with the music. The piano concerto emanating from the handheld radio has an anthropomorphic quality; we imagine the presence of a piano player in the desert and a quartet, the base of the cello stuck in the sand.

I sit on a towel across the sand, my eyes covered with sunglasses. I'm drinking from the bottom of the grapefruit juice.

"You drank all the juice," Grandma says.

"I was thirsty."

"You're always thirsty," Grandma says. "Maybe you've got diabetes."

I turn over on my stomach. The desert rays off the white sand enhance the heat across my body, naked from the torso up. "I'm a growing boy."

"They use the slow movement from Piano Concerto number Twenty-one in the delivery room," Grandma tells me. "To ease childbirth."

"I should call my mother," I say.

"She's probably playing Mao." Grandma gets up and rubs off all the lotion with a wet towel. She walks to the rear door of the camper to get her camera equipment ready for our shoot.

"You're being lazy," Grandma says. "You just sit in the sun."

"I need to relax."

"You're too tense. It's not normal for a boy your age."

I get up off the towel and shake the loose sand off my bare arms and legs.

"I'm ready," I tell Grandma.

It was the drug-taking hour, the plunger with an aperture. Yet Grandma's camera was as seductive as a ten-thousand-dollar bag of junk. The way the opening of the aperture lets in the light, the hologram of the camera reflecting the image, and the chemicals on the film—all this is not dissimilar to the right junk shot up a raw vein. Heroin is about letting in a different light, the kind that you have to surrender to, like in a good photograph. When I'm high, I'm making a statement, I'm seducing and directing the film. It's my photograph.

"I spent hours studying lilies." She brings out her prized Rolleiflex camera. It has taken pictures of all the glamorous fashion models in Paris, the staterooms and boudoirs of world leaders. The camera has been privileged to see the inside of brothels and opium huts on the Left Bank of Paris, a murder under a bridge on the Seine, Antonin Artaud passed out on the street from opium, and the illegal immigrants who live along the narrow passages of catacombs under Paris.

"I know the colors of orchids and pinks they don't have anymore," she tells me.

The way she holds that camera makes me feel safe. The click in the lens means she likes what she sees. I can see her pupils dilate if I stare at her lens long enough. Her red fingernails surround the body of the camera. It is a form of communication for us. She understands life through a photograph, and I was her study. Like Rodin's models. He fell in love with them.

I am preparing for a long session in the windswept heat of this parched ocean, wishing for something in the landscape that is the color of aquamarine so I could imagine water.

"What was Paris like in the forties?" I ask her, as she changes her 150-millimeter lens into a 50-millimeter lens so she can get tighter on my face.

"I was so drunk, I don't remember. I always had these hats on that blocked my view of everything." She places a light meter above my face.

Grandma and I traveled to Paris when I was twelve. What I remember about Paris is Grandma's camera. I understood Paris through the way Grandma framed the city.

I remember Grandma's quest for hats. She decided to do a portfolio on the hats of Paris. We traveled through most of our first three days in Paris in search of exotic headdresses. Some ladies danced on sidewalks in small hats that just covered their foreheads, suggesting Muslim veils. Other women wore broad-brimmed coolie hats made of straw and white ribbon. Grandma sat with them and discussed the arches in cathedrals while she photographed their conversations and covert thoughts.

When Grandma was searching for a picture we walked around Paris for ten hours. We never stopped. We walked from the Left Bank all the way to the far end of Paris at Sacre Coeur above the Pigalle district. She always walked ten paces ahead of me. I thought sometimes she forgot I was there. However, I followed in tow, standing behind her silently when she found a subject.

Grandma and I had taken a barge down the Seine. I studied the people on the boats. They thought about how the river turned silver at night and about cooking the fish they hoped to catch. I knew there were no fish in the Seine, but it was part of the day.

From the boat, I saw people sleeping on the banks, wearing *frontières* and striped kerchiefs. They sat on their belongings, all held in a pillow bag. These places had a pungent smell of formaldehyde.

Grandma took pictures of nuns in lace turbans. They mixed with the black of their gowns as they made their way silently through the city, with Christ dangling at their feet, held by a long silver chain. They held their heads as if posing for God.

In the twenties in Paris, Grandma said, ladies danced on the sidewalks, wore berets suggesting the Basques. Some men wore soft felt fedoras with crescent crowns and pinstriped suits of sober hues. Their hair was slicked back. These men had pencil-thin mustaches. It was swing music and trying to find a slow, slow, fast, fast.

* * *

"What do you remember about Paris?" I ask Grandma in the desert.

I look at the dried saguaro cactus, brown and shedding all its remaining green, the night-blooming cereus budding dead pink flowers along its spines, these cactuses perpendicular to the thick clusters of rich salty dirt under my feet, maybe the same as those found in the Sahara or Gobi.

"Morning light," Grandma said. "When I stood on the top of Notre Dame and took an aerial shot of Paris at dawn and the sky was an Aristotle blue," Grandma says. "Brassaï did Paris by night. I did Paris by dawn."

Grandma rolls film into her camera. She examines it as though it were a patient. She places her eye to the viewfinder, places the lens toward the sky, checks the internal light meter to make sure the needle is floating, and adjusts the speed to four hundred.

"Why do you take pictures?"

"To forget Hitler."

"I wonder what you must have been like?"

"I was in love with de Gaulle," Grandma tells me.

As she snaps the first photo in the desert sunrise—an entire body shot of me in shadow—I imagined her bent in shadows of doorways and brothels, a young Jewish French girl with the troops of Nazi soldiers making a presence in the town. She was wearing a long dress and a floppy sweater. Her eyes could have been white with hysteria as she sat behind shutters, waiting for another burst of shellfire. She carried needles and thread and sewed all afternoon with my great-grandmother.

They sat behind windows with broken glass, waiting, her socks protecting her from the cold, over which she wore her ballet shoes. Maybe her bangs crept out of her helmetlike felt cloche over bobbed hair, perfectly combed and black, the rest hidden underneath. She must have looked like a boy.

Grandma aims the camera at me. Grandma moves in closer. This time it is a shot from the torso up.

"We've got a good five hours of light," Grandma said.

"Can we have breaks?" I asked.

"We'll be done in four hours."

I regret to having committed to five hours of being the model. Now we are in our fourth hour of shooting and I'm exhausted. The arches in my feet are like sand. I realize this would be a good time for an adrenaline shot or speed. Neither of which is available in the Mojave desert.

"My feet hurt."

Grandma does not respond to me.

"Don't you have enough pictures of me?"

"I have to record memory," Grandma says. "That way I can take it with me when I leave. I've got to save each last frame."

"What are you going to take with you?" I ask. I move my face into profile.

"You. The desert. And Marlene Dietrich." Grandma is focusing the lens, opening the aperture to find a halo of white light.

Grandma points her finger at me, trying to get me to pose under a cactus. The sunlight burns my eyes. I have tears coming down my face. This process of being pinned into a photo is almost a form of strangulation. I focus on Grandma with her visions of Paris.

Grandma knew what she was doing when she talked about Paris and the past. This is how photographers communicate. They discuss their lives in order to get you to open up. They divulge their secrets to hear yours. This conversation is used as a sketch for the eventual photograph.

"I'm taking an inventory of time," Grandma tells me. "What do you want to put in the capsule?"

I would say, My father's nude body. The silent films of Léger and Eisenstein. Grandma and the desert.

"What's it going to be?" Grandma asks. "We're losing the light."

All my life, family communication has occurred visually. What I don't say she could see through her lens, the old truth that the camera never lies.

"I see the ocean and my father's bare back," I tell her.

"What else?"

"Running from my father's house at midnight," I say, as I stare directly at the lens. Grandma snaps the camera.

"Great picture."

Grandma knows what I would put in my capsule, but the picture would be the equal of my words. She knows the naked body scenario only through the tiny hole letting in light to the aperture and from the details I omit. It's the silent-picture truth. Grandma will make up in her head what I am thinking. Through the camera she will know about my father's house, my clothes shredded by my father's fingers, the blasted purple bougainvillea flanking the lattice on my father's porch.

As Grandma continues taking my picture, I tell her about when I was five, when Father's addictions began with the telephone calls at midnight.

"We communicated only by phone during the week," I tell Grandma.

"Where was your mother?" Grandma asks.

"Shooting."

"Was he high?"

"I think it was scotch and cocaine," I tell her.

"What about the phone?"

I look at Grandma and speak very fast and low. "We

would do it on the phone and I was my father's play doll."

Grandma lowers her camera. "I didn't get that shot."

I keep my head turned away from Grandma.

"What else happened?" Grandma's voice deepens. "It's never just a phone call."

I'm telling Grandma that Father took me apart and reordered my body parts. He wanted to change my gender.

"The body can pretend things for distant fathers," I say to Grandma.

"What else happened?" Grandma asks again.

"I don't remember," I say.

Thirty-six exposures have been completed. Grandma puts the finished film into a black canister. I knew she wanted three rolls out of this afternoon. She would not stop until it got dark. I couldn't wait to eat.

"Don't tell me you don't fucking remember," Grandma says.

"I went to his house on the weekends," I tell Grandma. "We did things for a couple of years." I sit under the tree in her search for more truth. The backdrop a barren landscape.

"What kind of things?" Grandma asks.

"You know."

Grandma continues to take pictures. I don't want to hurt Grandma, I know those Percodans and the other painkillers she had in the camper were for real. I regret telling her, and I don't know how to make it up. If I pretend I lied, that would not erase the pain of what I told her. I look over at the sand dunes shadowed in the cold morning light, and all I see in the distance are rattlesnake holes and rabbit footprints.

Grandma reveals her face and lets the camera hang around her neck. She places the lens cap over the lens.

"Does your mother know," Grandma asks, "as much as I do?"

I bury my face in my hands.

"How could she not know?" Grandma asks.

"Maybe she does?" I ask her. It begins to get hot and I take off my sweatshirt. "Or she doesn't?"

"Is this a story?" Grandma asks.

I don't answer the question. I look at the cliffs of the mountain. I have been in this pain before, but it was a scene in a movie I played in. The only things missing are the camera crew, lighting guys, and a painted backdrop. "I visited my father on the weekends. He'd lock me up in the basement for hours. It was usually the afternoons he'd come down in the basement to undress me. We did it on a chiropractic table he had set up. It was usually done to me with an object or himself." It occurs to me I'm forgetting the story as I tell it to Grandma. I ponder if by telling this story to Grandma I will leave behind that boy in the basement. "And I still have cut marks all along my legs and back."

"What about your father?"

"What father?"

"Have you talked to him?" she asks.

"He'd never admit it," I say. "I've written letters."

"Maybe you should talk to him?" Grandma advises tentatively, her voice cracking. "Maybe something can be resolved."

I move out from under the tree. "I don't think so."

"And your mother?"

I look the other direction.

"She should know," Grandma says.

"Never. I won't tell her."

"It's your mother. She needs to know."

I say nothing.

"I hope he drops dead," Grandma says. "I curse him."

I walk over to the cactus and position myself beside it,

move my legs in a plié and cheat toward the camera. The grazing sun is pounding on our backs, burning light spots into Grandma's lens.

"I want you to get this on film," I tell Grandma as I lift up my shirt. My back has various burn marks and blemishes I got from my father.

Grandma points the Rolleiflex at me again and I stare into its sacred lens, its butterfly openings. I open my eyes wide for the lens, letting color spill. I realize that this camera is the last hope for Grandma and me. I will use it as a tether back to life, and Grandma will use it as a window to exit through. Grandma wears a wide grin from below the body of the camera. I hear the camera shutter snap. The film begins to rewind itself. "The last exposure," Grandma says.

28

All I do is cry under the comforter in the motel tonight about that boy locked in dark rooms.

I was five years old when I first met my father. He was living in Malibu, on the Pacific Coast Highway, in a house the board of trustees of Notre Dame had lent him. Malibu was secluded from the rest of Los Angeles. It's a city without neighbors, communication, or my mother.

The first time I met him, the white clapboard house on a bluff represented freedom to me. This house faced the origami sea, its bay windows witness to a hundred forms of orange sun. I absorbed the air like a cotton ball, its fragrance in my pores, sterile and luxurious. My father had fields of sage surrounding his house, their purple heads violet velvet, all high enough to hide the life of the house's inhabitants.

The house was down a long driveway. My mother's driver took me to meet him, and we cruised around trying to find it. The house was nearly invisible from the road.

The driver glided down the path, and even at five I knew this house would be the beginning of suicides.

I was sitting in the back seat of his old yellow Bentley, concerned and doubting if he would accept me, searching for images of what he would be like, holding onto the steel ashtrays. I opened the leather pockets behind the seats and found pills in little plastic bags and silver antique canisters, the Hollywood trade papers alongside the mahogany paneling. The car a gigantic lemon cake, my father's moving chaise longue.

He created rituals around what he had me do. Always we drank carob milkshakes before. I knew when the refrigerator opened that it was close to the time when the stitches tightened.

I would watch him pull the gray shades down and then we would hide at the bottom of the house, in a dark bathroom.

He said, "Pretend you're a girl. Purse your lips." In that tiny room, my father's pants would fall down, and for me the idea of drowning became intoxicating, and I would act for him. I would put on Shanghai red lipstick.

"Speak with a lisp, be my daughter." My limbs turned inward and I would become his daughter.

My feet were bound in heels, tiny toes clasped in their leather corners. I wore a red silk dress with pleats in it. I would fantasize they were the hair on my legs. My knees locked in frenzy when my father entered me, as if the cartilage were disconnecting and my muscles were drops of acid. He always came on my back, unable to look at me. My back became a geisha girl, the skirt lifted high above the tailbone. I was unable to see the fluids, unsure of what it all looked like. My father became a skeleton, a machine.

These rituals went on for years. I was never sure of when the refrigerator might open. I did know there had to be sun. The sun gave him power. Afterward, I was not allowed to clean myself. I had to crawl into his bed and hold him, sticking to him like a termite, drying in his sweat, bleached and bonded.

We would sleep into night, pretending we were father and son.

"I'm not crying," I say when I call my mother from a wind-whipped pay phone down the road. 3 A.M. "I'm fine."

"Is she giving you drugs?"

"No."

"You've got a six A.M. call tomorrow."

"I know."

"Aren't you excited?"

I don't answer.

"You will be back in time?"

I feel a large pumping sensation through the temples. I reach to hang up the phone. "I'll be there."

"We're finally playing mother and son," she says.

We'll see, Grandma had said.

The loud crushing noise of the cat scan makes its way over to Grandma's head. She is strapped down on the platform, waiting to go inside the deep well of the X ray. Grandma is still swinging her arms up in the air and laughing as the machine makes its way over her entire body. Two doctors try to put her arms down and she slaps their hands away. Grandma goes on swinging her arms to the music.

I always go to Grace's apartment on Friday nights. I had given her some money I stole from my mother to get her own place. Grace shares an apartment in the La Brea Tar Pits Courtyard with two punk-rock girls who play in a band called Clit.

The La Brea complex is built in the center of the mid-Wilshire district, ten minutes west of Grandma's house. La Brea Courtyard is a gated area with ten highrises and three hundred homes built in Los Angeles in the early seventies that is supposed to be an urban utopia, complete with sub-terranean parking lots, large parks, and tall gates for security. The highrises are painted a dark shabby gray and have flat surfaces with perfect geometric-shaped windows and corners. It looks more like a prison. What is most appealing about it is that it's built over dead dinosaur bones.

I walk down the wide open streets with imported palm, maple, and oak trees that just hang over large empty expanses of clean-cut grass. All I hear is the echo of a fall wind. It's like an endangered rain forest, with all the animals gone.

Grace lives in Building One, apartment B1.

When I arrive, Grace is on the phone talking to a client.

She wears a black bustier, garter belt, and black high heels and carries a whip. On the phone, she is discussing her next appointment. Above her on the wall are five-by-seven portraits of her seven-year-old sister Camilla, who is dying of leukemia in Seattle, where she sends the money from her business every month. Grace's sister got the cancer from growing up living next to a chemical plant and in the water.

"You didn't call me Mistress Jessica," she says. "I'm going to really beat you up."

I sit leaning over the couch, watching her on the phone.

"I'm not tough enough?" she asks. "Next time," Grace says, "I'm going to do the fire and ice on you."

I look around the room. It's scattered with lace underwear, black nail polish, handcuffs, and an AA sobriety chip.

"And you can take out the pads I told you to wear," she tells him. "I'm not menstruating anymore."

Grace reaches over to hang up the phone.

"I didn't know you were in AA," I say. "How long have you been sober?"

"Next subject," she says.

Grace is getting her dungeon ready for her next visit. She is attaching handcuffs to the clothes bar.

"I've got a half hour," she tells me.

"I just came here to talk."

"Eighty bucks."

"I'm not paying anymore."

"Okay," she says. "Do you want to fuck me?"

"Fine," I say. "When?"

"Tonight," she tells me. "Where?" she asks.

"My mother's out of town," I say.

31

"I didn't know you were a virgin," I say.

Grace has screamed as I try to enter her tonight. So loud dogs barked.

"I haven't broken it yet," she says.

"You don't have sex with the others?" I ask.

"Not a chance," she says.

We have to wait, it's too painful. So we just rub against each other. And this feels safe for me. I don't give her too much.

When I come it's between the bedsheets and all over her palms. After, she goes to the bathroom and washes herself. She washes it off her palms, stomach, chest. She brushes her body intensely.

Later we sleep together, tightly knit into the bed, her clean and washed body against my stomach, me cradling her from behind.

The lights are out and my mother's house is empty. The lights are dimmed in the den, yellow fuses highlighting the corners in the walls.

I feel the first time is breaking your mother's cherry. Some trap that is now gone.

Later I start turning into the isolated characters in the Edward Hopper paintings. I move to the corner of the bed, away from her mineral scent and warmth, which gets insufferable. I pull my body up onto the frame of the bed.

"What's wrong?" she asks, her voice and eyes half asleep.

I answer, "Nothing."

She asks again, "Is it me?"

I get up and take all my wreckage: the underwear, jeans, socks. And I'm dressing some older person. I quickly gather the watch and shirt, touching the fabric as if they belonged to someone else. My arms feel wider and I sense in my chest some mistake of manhood, a false pride.

I can't equate sex and death, I realize, leaving my mother's bedroom. I have to wait until it's all over.

32

"I feel sick," I tell Grandma in the taxi the next day.

"What happened?" Grandma and I are going to stroll Hollywood Boulevard. Grandma put on her jewels before we left to promenade along Hollywood. She went to the vault at the bank and took out her tiny diamonds, seed pearls, and brooches and hid them under her coat as we took a taxi to Hollywood Boulevard.

"We had sex," I say, my voice stern. "But it wasn't sex. It was loud and wet." I look out the taxi window for explanations. "Sex is not what I expected it to be."

"She's that good?"

What did I not finish in the bedroom? I clasped the heavy acid in my stomach. "Can men lose their virginity?" I ask Grandma.

"Maybe you're too young," Grandma says.

"I think it felt too good." I look at the world enlarged around me, the buildings farther away. I feel one inch tall. "I don't think I can fall in love with anybody," I tell Grandma. "Not while you're alive."

Later, when Grandma and I are at Mann's Chinese, we stand

by Rita Hayworth's imprints and Grandma takes off her shoes to slip into the other woman's feet engraving. I lace my fingers across the large handwritten signature in cement and follow it as if it is a wave. Just as I felt in Laughlin, this Sunday with Grandma feels like being filmed by a camera. I feel as if I am something captured by a magnet.

When my mother's movies were hits, people came by in buses. My mother did not allow me outside without a chaperone. I looked out at the faces of people looking at my house from a tour bus, people who had traveled across the country from towns in Ohio and Nebraska. They flashed cameras at the window, and I just smiled. I never understood why they transported themselves to California to look at other people's lives. The way the bus made its slow turn onto our driveway as if they knew us, they wanted to have dinner here, they wanted to take our pictures home to their families. As loyal as they were, they wanted to steal something from us.

I would wear disguises to go out. I would dress as a little girl, and I pulled it off, sauntering down the driveway at age nine, unnoticed, like a scarved and hunched Marilyn Monroe. When I wanted to go to the movies, I wore warm hair curlers, dust coat, and a scarf around my head. I felt safe as a woman, considering my father wanted a girl.

All the Rita Hayworths in the world had to fake their exits and entrances, making it seem invisible, pretending nobody saw them.

We walk to the ice cream store, C. C. Brown's, down the block from Mann's Chinese on Hollywood Boulevard, where Grandma takes me after the movie on Sunday. This is where movie stars went after premieres. The white clapboard room is filled with jars of chocolate and molasses, below spinning ceiling fans. This restaurant implies Bourbon Street in New Orleans, with the French Quarter's pink brick shotgun houses or whiskey parlors. Grandma and I sit in high-backed black walnut booths eating ragtime chocolates. We are served high-butterfat ice cream topped with whipped cream and covered in fudge that turns into hard candy.

"Let's celebrate," Grandma says.

I am eating the last remains of the ice cream with hot fudge sauce. She waves her hand up in the air for service. "Let's pretend we're Carole Lombard and Clark Gable. We're going to the Roosevelt Hotel," Grandma says. "I'm going to show you Gable and Lombard's suite."

The waiter, in a white ice cream parlor uniform and apron, places a check in front of Grandma.

"Excuse me, sir. I would like to take your picture in exchange for your sundaes," Grandma says. "I'm the famous 'Highland of Hollywood.'"

Grandma takes out her business card and slips it into the waiter's palm.

"You're the one who took pictures of all the old famous people," the waiter says.

Grandma hands the empty ice cream dish to the waiter. She lifts the camera to frame him. "Get excited for the picture. Imagine you're serving Clark Gable and Carole Lombard. Perfect. Get more into it, open your eyes wide."

Grandma snaps five pictures. "Think of this as the serving of your life," she demands. "Consider, you'll never serve anyone as great as this. Give me that thrill."

Grandma finishes the last two head shots.

"You look ten years younger," Grandma tells the waiter. "I'll send you a print."

The waiter picks up the check and leaves with a sense that he is now a movie star. Grandma does not have to pay.

"We are Lombard and Gable." Grandma aims the lens at me.

I stare at the lens. Grandma snaps one last picture. She

rewinds the roll of film by hand on her old thirty-five millimeter camera.

We go across the street to the Hollywood Roosevelt
Hotel. Grandma gets the key to the Gable and Lombard
Suite from the hotel concierge. She tells them she is taking
pictures to document the place and the couple, saving last
articles.

A brass plaque outside the door reads LOMBARD AND
GABLE SUITE. Inside the two-story suite, on the fifteenth and
sixteenth floors, is a large panel of windows that overlook
Hollywood Boulevard. The room is designed with sterling
silver fixtures and maroon fabrics.

"This was all before the plane crash, of course."
Grandma is studying the color composition of the room.

I say nothing.

"They were very much in love," Grandma says.

Grandma takes out her light meter and starts scanning
the room for light. "Lombard died in a plane crash over the
desert. She was returning from entertaining the troops. All
of America mourned. I was in Paris among the Germans,
hiding, and even I heard about her."

I walk over and close the silk curtains to help Grandma
avoid reflections from her flashbulbs.

"Gable is why I came to America," Grandma explains. "I
was in France and I had to escape during the war. I had just
seen the movie *San Francisco*. The camaraderie between the
two men moved me so much, I decided to finish my studies
at Berkeley."

"What was Gable like?"

"The last gentleman," Grandma says. "Once his car had a
flat tire in the desert. I was just leaving the Racquet Club
and I saw him in the middle of the road, fixing his tire
while he waited for a tow truck. He let me have a private
sitting." Grandma continued scoping the space of the room.

"I had only twenty minutes," Grandma told me. "It turned out to be my best portrait."

Grandma puts the camera on her tripod.

"Gable and I love tulips." Grandma points to the fresh-cut tulips on the bureau. These look like Grandma. They are art deco, long-necked, red, and carefully laid out, as if sculpted into their long stems. They emit a toxic fragrance of lemon and honey.

"It was a secret affair they had. This was the room they escaped to," Grandma says. "He would comb her blond hair all night, staring above the city."

I sit on the bed staring up at the high-pitched beams with oil murals representing Botticelli's Venus painted across the ceiling.

"Heaven must be ten million hotel suites overlooking Hollywood Boulevard," I say. I slip between the sheets. "There are yellow silk sheets under here," I tell Grandma. "I feel like a gangster."

"All gangsters have yellow silk sheets," Grandma says.

A few hours later we sit talking in the penthouse roof garden. We have the whole city lit up below us at night, in our perimeter, overlooking it through the back of the Indian-red neon marquee of the Roosevelt Hotel, permanent red tint across our faces.

"I took pictures of Norma Jean down at that swimming pool." Grandma is staring over the ledge. She is quiet. "I have to pick out a grave," Grandma finally says.

33

It is evening, and I am searching for money for Grandma's grave. I am standing in front of my mother's house watching through the dark windows, not a trace of family in the house. The jasmine blooming outside in the wet night, the grass washed over from the morning rain, and the wet concrete all remind me of childhood, my mother and me dancing in the rain, unafraid of consequences.

The day I'm thinking of was gray-washed, with black slick asphalt oil and fallen cypress and palm leaves, and the chance of lightning in the humidity, although it was temporary, as the clouds started to part above the San Gabriel Mountains.

Mother put on Billie Holiday in the living room, musty and dark from the rain, and the sax and bass would filter out into the little courtyard of the house we lived in then, when we were without means. Mother wore a twenties vermilion silk dress, with pleated bottom and yellow gardenia print. Her hair got all wet, the long brown strands close to her neck. Mother's arms were so free they were able to reach out a long way when she spun me around in a circle, dancing under a rare somber sky.

The gates are locked, because I live with Grandma. I ring the intercom.

"What do you want?" she asks, her voice tense.

"I'm hungry," I tell her.

"Didn't they feed you on the set?" she yells back.

I pause and poke my hands into my ears while my mother's high-pitched voice screams on the speaker.

"You don't want to put on any weight." she says. "On camera you look ten pounds heavier."

"I can hear you," I tell her. "You don't have to yell."

When I was a child and I was hungry, I became the food. When my mother made me diet, wanted to thin me out even more, I cut out pieces of food in magazines and pasted them on my walls and stared at them when I was trying to fall asleep. I thought my red tricycle could turn to licorice.

Being hungry is like being at the end of time. Each spasm is a slow hallucination. I thought my arms were turning into plastic, that I would be stuffed into Zip-Lock bags, that I was cellophane. You want to kill yourself to quiet the pain, the loud noises in your head. I collected food from school and hid it from my mother. Apples and bananas, always under the bed.

A few moments later Eduardo, who doubles as my mother's new twenty-five-year-old Argentinian personal trainer and live-in boyfriend, comes down the driveway with food. He passes a baguette and a plate with several cubes of mozzarella through the wrought-iron bars. I grab for the basket he holds, filled with blueberry and carrot muffins.

I say nothing to him.

I sit on the curb eating the mozzarella spread across the center of the warm baguette. In the corner of my eye, I see the light on in my mother's bedroom and the shadow drifting back and forth between the pulled-down shades.

Did my mother ask Eduardo to bring the food or did Eduardo pity me? I need to believe, as I sit in the grass in front of the house, jeans wet, that she is getting better. It's very dangerous when my mother thinks I'm hostile to her. She takes that as a threat.

After a few moments I feel the gate creak open and then the warm brush of silk along my back. I know when my mother wears silk she is in a mood to be consoling.

"Don't put on too much," she tells me. "You're getting a double chin."

She offers me a slim peck on the check, like it never happened, and withdraws.

"What's happening?"

"I need money for Grandma's grave," I tell her.

"What do the doctors say?"

"They don't commit to anything," I say. "And she refuses to do any treatment," I say.

"She needs doctors who can help her."

"Grandma won't go back to the doctor," I tell her again. I show my mother a big brown envelope. "They did X rays. They found the cancer has traveled to her lungs and brain."

I pull from the envelope the large eleven-by-fourteen negatives. All I see are white smoke-filled sections and a rib cage.

"Is she taking pictures?" she asks.

"Yes," I say.

"She can't live without her camera!" Mother says. She rips up the X rays and throws them all over the grass.

"She doesn't have much time," I say.

"She's not going to die," my mother states. "It's not in her character." Nobody believes she is going to die, I realize, looking at my mother's stern face, having rendered a decision on mortal fate, the squandered gamma rays along the grass.

"Just to make her happy," I say. "We need to buy a

grave." I offer this suggestion to appease my mother.

"If it will make her happy, I'll give you some money," she says. Mother squats beside me and begins to pick at the cheese on my plate. The words that followed were plans. "You don't believe she is going to die?" It's the first time she's asked me the kind of question that makes me responsible for her.

"We can move to Paris," I say.

"I'd like to get old on a farm in the South of France like Brigitte Bardot," my mother tells me. "And eat lots of goat cheese."

"We could get a place in the Val de Loire," I suggest. "We could leave Los Angeles."

"And do what?" Mother asks. "I could never leave here."

"What about doing movies in France?"

"French cinema is dead. The only good thing about living in Paris is the fall fashion shows and Christian Dior."

Mother's face has a look of terror at the notion of leaving the Pacific Rim. "This will always be my home. As you know, I have trouble learning foreign languages. I can't even memorize my own lines."

I look down my mother's empty residential street as the lampposts begin to flicker on.

"If you do another movie," she says, "you'll be fine. You won't ever leave me," she says, her voice quavering. "And if you do, which you won't, I'll be fine."

"I'll take care of you," I say to her, against my own previous judgments.

"What will happen to us?" my mother asks. Her face is puzzled, drifting amid scenarios.

When I look at the night over Mother and me, brief hot breezes over her hair, her skin turning red, I believe that when Grandma dies, my mother and I will be the only two children left in the world. It is in that moment that I know we will have to find new ways to understand the universe when Grandma dies, and this will have to happen to us together, as a family.

"What about calling your father?" Mother asks. "He should at least talk to her."

"I've haven't tried to reach him," I say. "I think I need to see him." I get up off the grass and try to brush off the green stains on my pants. "Maybe I'll write a letter," I say.

"He'll call. He's a quarterback," Mother tells me. "He's always good for the last touchdown." My mother states these words with false assurance, her eyes determined; I can hear her mistrust in her voice, high pitched like a young girl's; she says what she says because of the parental agreement not to make a mistake in front of your child, to protect me, to ignore the mistake of picking the wrong father.

"What would I do if I saw my father?" I ask.

"How long has it been?" my mother asks.

"Five years," I say. "It's always felt like I've never actually met him."

"Don't bite your nails."

"I'll go visit him."

I try various words and phrases in my head of what will be the opening greetings or stories I want my father to tell me. When I see my father, the only thing I can think of to say or ask first is, "Are we just animals?"

My mother gets up from her spot on the grass and looks at me. "I've got to go get you a check for the grave."

"Are we just animals?" I ask

34

In November, Grandma and I walk toward the gates of the decayed Hollywood Cemetery. The cemetery is three blocks north of Grandma's house, located behind Paramount Studios. It's surrounded by a ten-foot gray wall with barbed wire across the top. The entrance is one large wrought-iron gate, decorated with curlicues. The cemetery is surrounded by barbed wire and electrodes, the gray stone walls covered in graffiti spray-painted in heliotrope and Day-Glo colors.

Grandma is making arrangements.

We walk down Gower Boulevard, which runs along the side of the cemetery, the autumn breeze bronzed and tumescent. Grandma places her hands on the brim of her hat in the wind, her mouth tightened, resisting any chill. She is silent today, possessed of a degree of peace, her expressions minimized and her voice calmed. It makes me uneasy to see Grandma this comfortable. This morning she sat outside in her gray coat, her black knee-high leather go-go boots crossed, her body crunched deep into her beach chair. I thought she must have questions about what would happen to my mother and me.

*   *   *

Before I moved in with Grandma, I was sitting in my mother's living room one night, the lamps reflecting on the black windows. They had just come back from the doctors. It was the night the doctors had given her a prognosis, told her about the traveling of the cancer. My mother was talking to the doctor on the phone, trying to negotiate a deal on time for cancer. She got off the phone and we kind of just stared at Grandma, the way people might at a dying dog that can't be helped. I felt Grandma had made twice as much space as usual between her and me, as if the prognosis made her feel contagious. I studied her pearl and gold ring, the white angora turtleneck sweater. I wanted to smother myself in the angora sweater, feel Grandma's breasts, arms, and whole weight against mine. Somehow hold on to her—her liver spots, long hands. When my mother announced each detail—chemotherapy, surgery, radiation, and homeopathy—it was like hearing gunshots; I could just hear the ringing sound of cancer in my ears. I was scared to grab her, as if she could be a pillar of salt, somebody's curse.

I went over to the white satin love seat in the corner of the living room, the seat narrow and tight. I asked for something cold to drink, with ice and citrus. They both remained calm, distilling the news, tried to mention the words softly, cutting any strong consonants. It wouldn't work, we all decided. It was terminal.

All the colors I saw that night were bright flesh tints. With shock, colors become compressed and inflated. I looked at the palm leaves in white ceramic pots in the corners, verdant and indiscreet, and the dead zebra under the Chinese mahogany wood table, pinned to the floor by the wide feet on the coffee table.

I walked over to the piano in the corner. I started with the only three keys I knew in the beginning of *Für Elise*, my hands dry against the rough ivory keys. Over and over I played the first three notes, quietly, as my mother and grandmother talked. It was the first time I could remember they didn't fight.

Standing at the piano I became more aware of my own body and felt not unlike a eunuch, somehow sexless and a little overweight, the stomach maybe a little too large for a young boy. I felt a surge of hate for my own body or any body that could die, for the disgust at decomposition, how it takes three days to a week and starts at the feet and works up to the upper body parts. I just kept the three notes going.

I turned around to look at my mother. She was wearing a cobalt-blue cotton Indian shirt and pants, and a blue satin half-turban with gold beads and an embroidered pattern in gold and bronze. Her skin was burnt sienna from the large amounts of a dark brown makeup base that she used all along her face, the blush across it and under her chin and deep into her chest an earth-tone red. She looked Spanish because her olive skin was accentuated by the red tones.

When we lived at the beach, Mother was always bronzed. Her hair fell down to her neck, black and sheer, and when she wore jeans and we played telephone with tin cans connected to a long yellow rope, I could always hear my mother's voice on the other side, accented by the rush of the tide and a gentle wind that usually we could find on the coast at sunset. The sand was damp from the incoming tide; it turned a mineral gray and almost glowed at those hours. My feet were making imprints in the sand, cold water on the outline of my ankles, even as I feared the white little crab bites. And I know my imagination started by staring at the ocean at sunset, playing phone with my mother. Remembering that day, I sat in my mother's house and contemplated whether I could play phone with the tin cans after Grandma died.

That day became an act of rearrangement. I walked through the living room, moving chairs into other places, shifting flowers and their colors into other vases. Staring through the emerald green vase on the living room table, so the living room looked like it was under water. Cleaning the dead sunflower petals and orchids off the table, anything that looked dead and left over. I walked over to the French windows in the living room, trying to open them, but they were shut by paint.

Later I went upstairs and into my bedroom, the fantasy room with the door that locks. I crawled into the sheets with my clothes on and could only think about sleeping out the numbness. I felt comfort in having my shoes and shirt still on. I looked at the movie posters on my wall. They had lost their vibrancy; someone had taken a large swan brush and painted over the exterior of my world.

The naked picture magazines I collected under my bed seemed tainted after the news. I felt guilty trying to sleep over them, tightly tucked in between the mattress and box springs. Every time I moved on the bed, I could hear them crease some naked body, its torso in vivid harsh colors, brushing against the bed. The pictorial layouts are taken with flash cameras, and the nakedness pops out like a comic strip against the very pink bodies. I wanted to throw them out, wondering if they could be the cause of cancer. I could not imagine an erection with the news. I reached over the side of my bed and pulled them out, flipping the glossy pages left and right, and I started to feel like vomiting. I shoved them back into the hiding place for another time. I was afraid I would get trapped in the pictures in the stories and scenarios I created, the way I always did. The favorite section with the most finger marks and creases on the page had become almost like tissue paper, the nipples crunched, the body looking like it was disfigured.

I heard the soft-spoken words down below creeping through the floor. I stared at the window, but it was black and I could only see a dense reflection of me in one square pane. My face and body made me look like something captured.

Grandma has hidden her leather purse inside a white plastic grocery bag that she uses for walking through Hollywood, tied in a knot around her wrist. Grandma always clasps her bag tightly, fearing someone will take it. Her purse preoccupies her. I think it could have to do with her family's money being taken in the war. Inside her bronze leather bag with snakeskin along the sides is makeup, lilac perfume, twenty dollars, her camera, a separate flash, a white rabbit's foot on a key chain, and her dried papaya and apples in a plastic sandwich bag. Grandma is wearing a lemon yellow rayon blouse and pants with gold square buttons. A white lace hat flops into her eyes and around her drooping pearl earrings.

We head toward my mother, waiting at the front entrance. "In order to be buried at Hollywood Memorial, you must know someone here," Grandma told me. "Dead or alive."

"I should have been told about the desert. I nearly had a heart attack," my mother frantically says to Grandma. "I even called the police." Grandma ignores my mother and continues walking.

"He could have got sick before his shoot," she says. "He's never allowed on vacations before a good scene."

"He needs to get away from Hollywood," Grandma says. "Fly from the nest, spread his wings a bit."

"He's got asthma. He could have had an attack," Mother adds.

"What are you doing here?" Grandma asks.

"We're making plans," my mother says.

"I don't need you here. You make me nervous."

"There's only a few plots left in the cemetery," my mother says. "Where do you want to be buried?"

"I decided it's not chic enough to be buried. I want to be cremated." Grandma continues walking into the cemetery.

"You have to be buried, you can't be cremated." My mother rushes forward to catch up with her.

"Leave me alone."

"It's against the Jewish Law."

"I'm a communist now," Grandma answers.

My mother goes to the office to make arrangements. Grandma and I walk around the cemetery. I speculate as to whether Heaven was like the Hollywood Cemetery or maybe Père-Lachaise.

"Even the palm trees have cancer," Grandma says.

We walk among toppled gravestones.

"Most of the people here were buried in the forties or fifties. In the forties, they built shrines to movie stars. They were divine Greek gods."

The cemetery has become so crowded that they actually piled people on top of one another. Everywhere are deserted gargantuan art deco monuments tipped over on the curb, engraved with names like Valentino, Karloff, and Clara Bow.

Grandma is standing in front of Valentino's tomb. It is green from salt deposits, a one-story tomb made of marble with courtyard gates at the entrance. "If you listen hard enough, you can hear the faint sound of Rudolph Valentino dancing the tango," Grandma says. "And then raping a girl."

We walk inside the small atrium inside the tomb. Inside it is black lead, except for a tiny stained glass window high-lighting Grandma's tangerine orange hair and aristocratic neck. The walls are no taller than six feet. Valentino lies in a vault behind a glass wall with a bronze plaque across the space in the pink marble wall.

"I want to be cremated and have my ashes spread along the desert," Grandma says. "When they cremate me, I want to be wearing my green taffeta dress with the emerald sequined buttons."

Her voice is confidential, signaling her trust in me. As she draws close to me, I feel her warm breath in between the words, smell the haze of lilacs on her neck.

"You're not going to die," I tell Grandma. Those are the first words I can utter, breaking the fourth wall. "You're not allowed."

"Leave me alone," she says.

Grandma stares through the shaft of light.

"There's something we can do. We can go to Mexico. They have special medicine. We can do the surgery. I know we can cure it."

"I don't care."

"I don't want you to die. You have to do the radiation or the therapy. I read about this healer in Mexico. He's healed people with cancer."

"I don't want to talk about it anymore."

"I want to talk about it. Where do I go when you die?" I say, throwing the gate open on the tomb. "You can't fucking be my mother and then leave me. I'm not some invisible person." I pace the tomb. "Another object in your camera. I'm your grandson and you owe it to me to stay alive." I say, as I start kicking my feet into the walls.

Grandma moves around in a circle in the tomb.

"I don't even know where you'll be," I say.

"They play black-and-white classics all day," Grandma tells me. "And classical music. Strauss, endless waltzes."

"What about my mother?" I ask Grandma.

"It's like dealing with a hurricane," Grandma says. "Just try be good to each other."

"I'll never again see your red hair. The beehive hairdo.

Your liver-spotted hands." I sit on the ground, the tips of my hair wet, my hands red. I put them over my face. "The way your profile looks in silhouette," I continue this litany.

Grandma cannot look at me. Her stare is eastward, out to the light.

"The way you smile when the apple pie is finished and warm."

"You've got pictures," Grandma says, leaning in closer, letting the last light in.

I crouch to the bottom of the floor, as the salt burns stain my cheek. I wipe the sour wet spots on my lips across my chin and arms, stinging broken skin.

"I remember a director telling me I could become a great actor because I held back the crying in a scene for a movie. He said I held back the tears with pride." I don't know what I am saying but I keep talking. "Why did I hold back?" I ask Grandma.

35

When I'm outside, I like to be high. It is now 9 A.M. and we're shooting on a mountaintop. It's the scene where the vampires come back to life. The high travels with me, suggestions of a better life; how I think my father would like to see me.

36

I walk into Grandma's hospital room, where she is sleeping with a handkerchief around her head, and look over her whole body. Her arms are bruised and covered with bandages. The nurses have her strapped down and tied to the bedposts.

"Grandma. It's Jordan."

Grandma moves, half groggy in her sleep. "They've got me all tied up."

I begin to untie the wraps on her arms. Grandma slowly moves her hands and leaves them up in the air.

"How do you feel?" I ask.

"Where are my negatives?"

"I have them. Don't worry. No one is going to take them."

"Make sure you hide them. They're going to take them."

"No one is going to take them." I hold Grandma's hand tightly.

"I want to get out of here," Grandma tells me.

37

By December Grandma's cancer has metastasized from the lungs into the bloodstream.

We get Grandma out of the hospital. I pull out all the tubes and heart monitor wires. Grandma still has her IV bag. In one month, her health has declined badly. I have to put her into a wheelchair, under a wool blanket, and wheel her out of the hospital. My mother's classic Mercedes is waiting for us outside.

"How did you get me out of there?" Grandma's voice is hoarse.

"We bribed them," my mother says.

"I don't think they even noticed," I tell her.

"This reminds me of when you took me out of that psych ward in Camarillo," Mother says.

"You were never in a psych ward," Grandma says.

"I remember I was twelve years old and you let them put me away. And you just sent me chocolate from your good life in Europe."

"I don't remember," Grandma says.

"Can we forget the past?" I ask.

"She's a liar," my mother says.

"Can we just pretend to be a family? Only for forty-eight hours. As an experiment, let's try not to fight. A biological quantum leap."

"Will you ever forgive me?" Grandma asks my mother.

"I have nothing to forgive. I don't know what you're talking about," my mother says.

I gather Grandma into my arms and use strength I didn't know my arms possessed to lift her slowly into the passenger seat and arrange her stiff bones on cushions. When I touch her arms, they are freezing. Grandma is vanishing. "Where do you want to go?" I ask her.

"Paris." Grandma slowly lies back.

"You have no lipstick on," says my mother, turning from the steering wheel to Grandma. She opens her bag and takes out a tube of her burnt sienna lipstick. Grandma reaches tentatively to open the front visor mirror, slowly making out her thinned features.

Grandma takes the lipstick and spreads the color around the tip of her wrist and hand. Then, using the lip liner, she starts to outline her lips.

"You're doing it crooked," my mother says. She leans over and turns Grandma's head around to face her, takes the thin pencil, and starts to draw around the creased line of Grandma's mouth.

"We're taking you to the *Queen Mary*," my mother says. "It will be as close as we can get to Paris." She leans away, satisfied with the outline of Grandma's lips.

"I want a suite," Grandma says. She kisses her two lips together and smoothes out the lipstick around the rest of her mouth.

"You've got it all around your chin." Again my mother leans over and with her thumb and index finger tries to blot out the lipstick mark, rubbing it deeper into Grandma's skin, making it disappear.

I look out at the sky in dusk, hoping we can make it to the *Queen Mary* before night completely falls. I still smell the ammonia and antiseptics they use on the floors and walls on the sixth floor, the dying floor of Cedars Sinai Hospital. It is more like a hotel with suites, so families can sleep on the pull-out couches in the hospital rooms. In the waiting room is a three-foot glass ball with neon orange streaks running through the center, sitting up against a window over the city. I gazed through the colored glass overlooking the city in an orange blossom death, reminding me of the colored lenses Grandma gave me. My mother starts the ignition, and I try to think of colors as we get closer to our made-up Paris.

The *Queen Mary* is a floating ghost, docked in Long Beach Harbor, her metal frame being eaten away by tourists and toxic water. It has the largest dining room ever built on a ship, a football field of wood from fifty-six countries all belonging to the British Empire. Every animal was taken aboard alive and then killed and eaten on this ship—it was a floating butcher shop. The dining room had throw-up stains, so when the ship went to war in 1940 they built new floors out of cork and linoleum. Two thousand ate here in the Second World War. Grandma tells me all this in the car.

We advance Grandma down the crooked hallways, all curved, so the ship wouldn't crack in a wreck. Years ago, Grandma tells us, there was more luggage than people on this ship. Each class came in through a different entrance. People came on the ship because they wanted to see celebrities, spill coffee on Clark Gable or Myrna Loy. To the right of our suite is the passageway to the indoor swimming pool for the first-class passengers, now dry, empty. The third-class passengers got to swim there during teatime. When the elite returned, the pool had to be emptied and refilled, at twenty-three gallons a minute; the first-class passengers were afraid of catching a third-class disease. Grandma told me there was no more mother-of-pearl on the ceiling, because it had been stolen by soldiers for poker.

The room was King Edward VIII's quarters. I use my cash from a residual check to pay for it. I told my mom I wanted to pay for Grandma's last trip. There are mirrors everywhere, so we won't feel claustrophobic, martini glasses and a shaker on the vanity. I think perhaps her tumors will leave her at the dock.

I lift Grandma onto the bed. It is easy. She collapses into the bedding, nearly asleep, twisted on her side, moving her punctured veins along the bed. She looks like a flood victim, trying to hold on to something. I arrange the arm that is still attached to the IV. We order from room service a bucket of ice and chop the cubes up into tiny slivers to give to Grandma for her dry throat. The ice was also used as food. I apply Q-tips with lemon for her dry mouth and throat. Grandma's voice is like sandpaper. I give her chips of ice. She can't eat anything more.

My mother sits in the corner of the room, talking on the phone to a press agent regarding a press release for Grandma's obituary. "I want it in *The New York Times* and *Los Angeles Times*," Mother says. "And a full-scale picture of her. She deserves at least four columns."

I believe Grandma is unaware of my mother's hushed telephone call in the corner. "It's a little premature," I mutter to my mother.

"These things have to be prepared in advance, otherwise we'll lose space," Mother tells me.

"I'm going to throw up."

"You've never understood the mechanics of good business."

"Grandma's death is not business."

"We are people made by the entertainment business, and we will die with good publicity."

"Let the captain know I'm here," Grandma says to us.

The ship doesn't have a real captain any more, only an actor pretending he knows about the route the cruise would take, the gargantuan engines and their operations. We are not going anywhere. We are minus one hundred and sixty thousand horsepower.

A few hours later I get Grandma ready for our stroll around the ship. On the dressing table is a bottle of champagne in a bucket of ice, sent by the captain.

"Don't let them see me like this," Grandma says. "I need to get made up."

My grandmother and my mother sit side by side, staring into the same mirror, putting on their makeup like showgirls getting ready to perform in Las Vegas.

I had brought Grandma's long indigo silk dress with sleeves that dipped to the floor. Grandma rips out the IV attached to her left arm so the dress can fit.

"What are you doing?" I ask.

"It's uncomfortable," Grandma says.

"Let her do what she wants!" Mother says, applying powder to her neck.

"Pass me my bag," Grandma says.

I pass her the camera bag and Grandma searches it. She pulls out a tinfoil package and hands it to me.

"Would you roll this for me?" Grandma asks.

"Are you sure this is all right?"

"It'll make you a man," Grandma says. I look at my mother in the mirror. She just shrugs.

A few minutes later, Grandma is painting her lips again, the joint held between them.

We all get stoned.

I take the stick from her and apply desert-orange lipstick

across her lips. Her eyes are closed. I place mascara along her eyelids.

"I wonder if anybody is here from the original crew," Grandma says, laughing out loud, inhaling the smoke from marijuana sifting above the air in the room.

Grandma's face is completely white, but I color it in with base and a sponge, covering up the scabs and liver spots. I can tell from how she moves, her hands groping for objects, feeling them out, that her eyesight is nearly gone. She can barely see her reflection in the mirror. She trusts me to present her.

Grandma loves to have her hair in a beehive. The hair is too thin to comb. I roll the long hair up and fold it over, fastening it with bobby pins. I spray her jasmine perfume across the neckline. When I paint her nails red, her arms are limp, as light as cotton.

"Don't forget to tell them I sailed on this ship in its heyday," Grandma tells me. The words have become barely audible.

"I will tell them Paris was Grandma," I say, my voice lowered.

I pin her diamond brooch to the left corner of the dress. I am wearing my black tuxedo.

I wriggle in to sit in the middle of the vanity seat, between my grandmother and my mother, talking to their faces in the mirror. "What does the end of time look like?" I ask Grandma

"It's infinity, time bends backwards," Grandma says. "Pass me the gold eyeshadow."

"The end of time is giving birth to a child," my mother says. "When you become a mother, time stops."

"What do you know about motherhood?" Grandma says.

"He's my child," Mother says.

"You didn't know how to raise him."

"I created him."

"When were you there?" Grandma asks.

"When I was pregnant with you at the beach," my mother says to my reflection, "I painted watercolors and just read. I painted images of what I thought my child would be."

"Where was Dad?" I ask.

"Who knew?" my mother says. "At night I called various hotels, trying to find out if he was sleeping with that actress."

"He'll always be a small-town hypocrite," Grandma adds.

I take a gardenia out of the bowl on the vanity and bobby-pin it into Grandma's hair, the white leaves and green stem fitted tightly behind her ear.

"He just planted the seed at that point. And that's all that mattered," Mother says, squinting for effect. "Grandma and I brought you into this world."

"He was good for his dick," Grandma says.

"That's all," my mother adds.

Mother starts to cough, wearing out the novelty of a cigarette. She just drains the smoke into her mouth, not inhaling and quickly letting the smoke right out, suggesting a high school girl's first cigarette in the bathroom, trying to be bad with blushing skin and giggles. "Grandma would drive down to the beach and make me eggplant. Fried eggplant, sautéed eggplant, any kind of eggplant," Mother continues.

"Your father didn't know what to do in Hollywood. He drank too much and wasn't made for warm weather," Grandma says to me. "Where is the eyeliner?" Her hand flutters over the cosmetics.

"Who needs men?" my mother says.

"They're all lousy," Grandma says. "All they want is to get in your pants."

Looking at them, sleek actress and vanishing dying

woman, I try to see them at the beach, at the tideline waiting for my arrival. The two women ushering in the boy.

"And we're still a family," my mother says.

My mother and I wheel Grandma onto the third-floor deck. Grandma has a wool blanket over her dress. She is bundled up for the cold. Salt mist coats her skin.

I stare at the muted coastline. We were facing the wrong ocean on an immovable boat. Maybe we could make this the Moulin Rouge.

I have brought the champagne with me in a bucket of ice. I place the three crystal long-necked glasses on the railing of the ship.

I look at the diamond brooch the size of my palm, on Grandma, fastened to her dress.

I touch the clumps of hair she had left that I had arranged, little dyed bunches of orange.

On the deck, I could hear the trumpets from the swing band in the ballroom. Through the swing music Grandma talked. Grandma lifted her champagne glass high into the air and we toasted, as the band played "Moonlight Serenade."

I watch my mother on her third glass of champagne. She never drinks.

"I can feel it killing me," Grandma says. "Give me some champagne."

"Should we make a toast?" I hand the glass to Grandma.

"To Mao," Grandma says.

"To obsession," My mother says.

"To my father," I say.

"Anything else?" my mother asks.

"To glamour," I say.

We toast.

38

"I'm tired of having to look beautiful," my mother says, as she smears red lipstick across her face on our second night on the *Queen Mary*.

I realize my mother is drunk and she's making a list of the people who wronged her.

"Put the lipstick on," Grandma says.

"I don't want to look beautiful, Mother," she says. "Not for you. Not for the studios. Not even for Eduardo at home."

"When are you getting rid of him?"

"When I am good and ready."

"We're not going to dinner until you put the lipstick and rest of the makeup on," Grandma says, her voice raised.

"I'm not one of your models."

"You have no respect." Grandma raises her hand in a clenched fist. "Get dressed and put your face on."

Mother gets up from the vanity and turns to Grandma's reflection in the mirror. "All my life I've tried to look beautiful for you, Mother. For the cameras. For the publicity stills. Is there any redemption in beauty?" Mother stares into the mirror and starts teasing her hair into wild streaks. "Since I was a child you've sent me to hair colorists, stylist, dentists, manicurists, and even surgeons."

"You had crooked teeth," Grandma tells Mother.

"Jordan, I was just her trophy. She never gave a shit about me."

"I'm trying not to listen," I say.

"Don't be such a square."

"Grandma is dying."

"All of you go to hell," Grandma says.

My mother reaches over and starts to place blush all over her face and clothes and all over Grandma's clothes and forehead.

"What are you doing?" Grandma's voice yells, high pitched.

"How about all those nights in Monte Carlo you called me from another man's hotel."

"I don't know what you're talking about," Grandma says, turning her eyes away from my mother.

"I've been wronged by you from the beginning," Mother says.

"I've done everything to help you."

"What about the foster homes, the hospitals?"

"I didn't have money. They were just trying to help."

"I was wronged by the doctors in the hospital you sent me to." Mother draws mascara across her face in sporadic lines.

"I don't want to hear this." Grandma covers her ears.

"I was locked in a little room they gave me. The doctors would come in late at night and each one of them would take turns with me."

"Stop it!" Grandma starts to yell at the top of her lungs, covering her ears. "Stop it, stop it."

Mother walks over face to face with Grandma's reflection in the mirror.

"Fucking gigolos in France and Monte Carlo were more important than your own daughter. It was more important for you to take pictures of naked women than to be a mother to your daughter while she was in a hospital." Grandma reaches over like a thunderbolt and slaps my mother across the face. The sound of skin snapping echoes throughout the hotel suite.

I only hear the sound of fabric moving around. I look at my mother looming in the background with a red, stunned face.

"Now it doesn't matter," Mother says. "It's all over."

My mother walks out of the hotel room.

"She'll be back," Grandma says.

39

"You're only twenty percent there," my agent, Stu, tells me on the phone. "The other actors are seventy percent. That's what I was told."

"What about all the scenes I shot?" I say.

"They're going to cut down the character in the movie and reshoot all the scenes."

"How are we equating an acting performance with mathematics?" I ask. "I'm not replaceable," I say to Stu.

"The door's closed but not shut."

"What else is wrong?"

"You haven't shown up on the set," he tells me. "And when you do show up, you're on smack."

"I can't help it," I tell him. "My grandmother is dying."

"That doesn't matter in Hollywood," my agent tells me.

"Fuck them," I say. "I have lawyers."

"For your information," Stu tells me, "it's our policy not to do depositions in this kind of case." Stu takes a long pause. "The other agents feel we aren't best able to meet your needs anymore," Stu tells me. "We're letting you go."

"Is that all?" I ask.

"They need their wardrobe back," Stu says.

40

Today I'll quit. It's been four days since the last hit.

In Grandma's kitchen, the knife for cutting the apple pie has an immeasurable appeal. I can see myself from the outside, holding rags, trying to stanch the bleeding. It has already happened. So I always keep the knife out, assuming I've cut the veins. I discover sweet liquors: brandy, whiskey, and rum. I wish for higher altitudes to quicken the high. I contemplate how good it would be to be drunk in the Andes.

Grandma is back in the hospital. My mother and I debate what liquids to give her in the IV. She has somewhere between two to three weeks left.

I cannot breathe in Los Angeles during December. Santa Anas cave in the opaque blue skies like a dust bowl carrying pollen. My eyes drip water.

I hear the shuddering of Santa Anas at midnight. I have put latches on the French windows and covered the cracked glass. I stuff broken windows with scarves and rags, trying to muffle the sound of wind. I put comforters over my head and sleep like an Eskimo, wrapping my body parts in thermals and thick socks.

I am walking to Mann's Chinese Theater the next morning still wrapped in warm clothes, even though the lightboard sign above the bank displays 72 degrees. I do not know the difference between actual climate and the chills from withdrawls.

Mann's Chinese Theater is one more version of what Heaven might be like, a bronze building with curves and points to chase away the bad spirits and large silver screens playing black-and-white classics all day long. Or so Grandma would have told me.

I go up to the red-carpeted entrance used for premieres. Its wings are clipped, and the bronze temple has fallen into desuetude. I know how crack, black beauties, and heroin are readily available around the corner from the theater up Orange Street.

I make my way over to a water fountain in the corner of the theater and search deep into my pockets for the pills I took from Grandma's medicine cabinet.

Barbiturates make your heart stop faster. It's the fastest way to unconsciousness.

Suicide is business. I think of where to put the letter. I have listed assets, banks, and lawyers.

At the water fountain, I hold twenty of these orange capsules. They feel very cold in my hand, I quickly ingest the Seconal and codeine.

I stare at Rita Hayworth's imprints. Grandma took her picture at the Racquet Club in Palm Springs in 1956. Rita was lying down on a diving board over the Olympic-size swimming pool. Her complexion was highlighted by a serene yellow, but I could see beyond her veneer that she was on tranquilizers.

We were both molested children. We both lived in Hollywood, where you surrender the past in order to become famous. Fame is the memory-loss drug. The equation you strive for, becoming famous, is what to take with you and what you leave behind.

What are the effects of the big pills of forgetting? She and I both had fathers who enjoyed our bodies and left us with detailed descriptions of what they had done to us. I understand Rita Hayworth's Alzheimer's, why she had so much to forget. After incest, you fall into deep unconsciousness. The interior of a clock mismanaged, springs cut open like veins.

I look for C. C. Brown's, thinking an ice cream sundae will take away the suicide taste. All around, and the landscape becomes a form of medication. As I walk down Hollywood Boulevard, I think my suicide is contagious. I walk toward the Hollywood Roosevelt and know I am spreading something. I can't shake the feeling of being infectious.

I get to a phone booth and call my mother and tell her I've taken two bottles' worth of coedine and Seconal.

"You're grounded," she says over the phone. My hands shake, holding the plastic phone outside of C. C. Brown's, and I can barely stand up.

"Why don't you get in an ambulance!" she yells into the phone.

I don't know if I should walk away or walk toward my grandmother's house.

"They should put you away!" she yells.

I just hang up the phone and begin moving, my breathing short.

I think how Grace sends me letters. It's the only girl I know outside of this world. I often take the letters and put them in drawers and hide them from myself. I want to call her. Would she take my call now?

Walking toward the ice cream store, I try to inhale and exhale, my chest tight.

I am five blocks north of Grandma's home. I feel no circulation in my body. There is a coldness along the rim of my mouth. I am starting to hyperventilate.

A young girl approaches me. She thrusts a blank piece of paper at me. "Sign it. We know who you are." She is heavy-set, with purple hair and a camera around her neck. "Don't try to hide," she says, and my knees get even weaker.

"I can't breathe," I let the girl know, as she shakes the paper at me.

"You always die in your movies, and you're still alive." The girl's face goes into fast forward, and I slowly feel the ground below me getting closer.

I turn my back on her and everything begins to fade. I look for my footing as she starts to take pictures of me.

I turn around and start to lunge for her, I try to swing my arms at her and rip the camera away but everything starts to go out of focus. I take the bottles out of my pocket and dart them at her and her family.

I hesitantly search for my balance and then crumble onto the Hollywood Walk of Fame, holding tightly to my pills.

And the 2.4 grams of codeine and sleeping pills roll out of my hands. My palm is empty. I look at the orange and white capsules squandered along my body.

Suicide loses its glamour on Hollywood Boulevard. The cold granite floor is against my back. My eyesight is out of focus, and I begin to throw up on the street and feel a warm urination between my thighs.

The group around me includes tourists and homeless people with alcohol breath, soiled clothes, and lost teeth.

We are a common denominator on the ground, I learn from suicide.

I hear a faint siren coming for somebody. I'm trying to smile for the cameras and the crowd roars, waiting for me to be strapped into the gurney, the fast paramedics. My ears absorb the scattered foreign languages above my slow death, all in foreign whispers, and I cannot understand the words.

41

They pumped my stomach and found traces of speed, morphine, codeine, and Seconal in my body. My mother hammered in nails against the opening of the windows, so I can't jump out. All sharp objects, including razors, knives, pencils, nail files, and anything else I can kill myself with, are taken from around the house and locked up in a storage bin. Again, this house was unobtainable to me and had locks to all forms of food or metal.

I slip on my burgundy silk bathrobe, pretending to be Hugh Hefner on my fifth day of withdrawl.

In the living room, the pink Christmas tree is lit. Unwrapped gifts in red paper surround the bottom of the tree. On the stereo, Nat King Cole is singing "O Little Town of Bethlehem."

As I walk into my mother's den, I look at the framed cover of *Time* magazine, with my father in his football workout jersey, number 34, from when he played quarterback for Notre Dame. In the picture, he is holding the Heisman Trophy he won in 1974. Now the trophy sits on the mantel in the living room.

I write my father a suicide note. I tear up all the family

albums and rip apart pictures with him and I send them to him. I create a Care package and a litany of anger. I wrap these gifts in Christmas paper, as if they are found treasures, something valuable and eternal. These are images of the Pacific Ocean when I was nine and we were collecting abalone shells, royal blue with a soft skin interior, dead sea life, starfish, tangled seaweed. Lost weekends with my father, all trapped in photo albums. I cut them up with razor blades, like a piece of his skin.

I go into my mother's kitchen. I find an ax for splitting wood for the fireplace—it is a weapon, she must have thought, too large to do me harm or else she just forgot—and split open the combination lock on her refrigerator. I eat a fruit tart, custard underneath, and thick almond crust. I imagine I'm with Grandma, eating her complex apple pies all made for me.

42

It's 4 A.M. and I hear below the slow brushing of water washing the pruned roses in my mother's garden. Naked and wet, they are waiting for spring, with cut limbs, dark green stems, and traces of yellow and fuchsia petals in the cold muddy puddles. This winter, Mother's rose garden is obsolete.

My bedroom door swings open. I can hear high heels carving into the pile, ripping the threads out of the hand-woven wool carpet. The shoes make their way to my bed.

"Get up," Mother says.

The ceiling light is turned on. The room turns bright yellow with the shock of light. Mother's heavy breath falls all over my pillow. The covers are drenched in sweat from the night.

"The locks have been broken on the refrigerator," Mother tells me. She is wearing her black lace mourning dress with the black ribbon.

"Why are you wearing a black ribbon?"

"Just in case," she tells me.

"Grandma's not even dead."

"It could happen any time. They say a month or a few weeks." Mother's voice is loud and impatient. "And she won't die."

Mother stares at me, her pupils dilated, rings under her eyes. It's not a drunken gaze but a look she acquired from twelve hours on the set, Grandma in the hospital, and a suicidal junkie son.

"I was hungry," I say.

"Where's the carving knife?" Mother asks.

"It was just a custard pie," I tell her. "That's all I cut. I didn't carve up myself."

Mother turns on the closet light and starts putting my clothes into a black valise. She throws each of my shirts, jeans, and socks into a suitase, looking for indications of suicide objects.

"You broke the rules," Mother says.

She is filling the luggage with my father's football trophies.

"What are you doing with those trophies?" I say.

"I don't trust you," she tells me. "You could get violent."

Each one flashes against the light as it tumbles into the valise, dropping gum wrappers, roach clips, and pens out of their loving cups. Mother takes the wire hangers in her hands, feels the sharp edges of the tips, and decides to put them in the suitcase too.

"They're my trophies," I say. "He is my father." I get up from the drenched sheets and rush to my mother. "I earned them," I say.

"You're only the son." She grabs the valise harder to pull it from my grip. "I was the wife."

"He loves me more."

"He does not. He slept with me."

"And me too."

"Liar," she says.

Mother goes through the lining of the bed and under the covers. She throws the mattress onto the ground, searching for something razor sharp. Mother grabs the sheets off the bed and rolls them up into a creased shaped ball.

"I'm taking these away," she says. "You could strangle yourself with these."

I sit down on the bare mattress against the garnet cotton and polyester.

"How could you say something like that?" she asks. "He's not that bad."

"I know what is the nature of evil."

"In what way?" Mother asks me.

"I would wait for presents we had bought to be wrapped for Christmas and Father would take me into the alley in the car outside of the store," I tell her.

I say everything I couldn't before about the car motor still running in the alley. The shiny keys hanging from the ignition tickling my cheek. My head below into the driver's seat, nestled between his lap and blue jeans, my head bumping up against the steering wheel with each movement.

My father's hand shaking as he turned the radio dial, passing through Bartók and Mahler and finding a rare Rolling Stones live cut from the seventies. The drum beat, the tamborines and the echo from the stadium-hall recording that flood my ears and the car. "Listen to that segue," my father said.

The gift-wrapped presents thumped against the trunk as we drove home. Some were piled high in the back seat, wrapped in pink tissue paper and white satin bows and obscuring the rearview window.

In my mother's contorted face is the sense that she believes me but holds back.

"He left marks," I say. A brine stain across the winged collar on my shirt and tie. How I used my cuffs to wipe away his body all over me. "And when we came home, I wasn't your son," I tell her. "I was a concubine of my father's."

All that Christmas, I thought about the alley with its dark gray walls off Hollywood Boulevard that I stared at with my father's hands all around the bottom of my back.

My mother stands by the open window, her face highlighted by the outside lamppost, her face making shadows on the window screen.

"Does Grandma know?" my mother asks.

"Yes."

"You told her first!" My mother's voice faint and high. "He took my son away?" Mother asks herself. "I'll kill him."

She begins throwing the trophies out the window. She grabs one trophy and hurls it through a closed window. The glass shards rip through the air.

"That feels better," my mother says. "I have to get my aggression out."

"Only if I turn around long enough do I see it," I say, my voice becoming stronger.

"What did he take from you?" My mother's voice becomes concentrated.

"Only parts of my body were taken. Not the whole of me."

"I'm going to take a gun and point it at his head and blow his brains out."

"I've lived in a crazy world because that's where my father left me. And the only way I've learned to be sane in this world is with Grandma." My voice is low and cracks. I tell my mother, leaning against the coolness of the walls, "I'm looking for logical reasons for why I should be sane."

"Kill him," mother says, her voice catatonic.

43

The rules of escape from Los Angeles are filled with quick calculations. I have to be careful, because my mother could track me here and blockade my journey to see my father.

There is a state of grace when you have someone who knows your itinerary, flight arrival, and departure. Somehow they even show up at the boarding gate when you arrive. On the other hand, I must not forget, there are some who don't show up after you've arrived.

I spend two hours waiting at the downtown Los Angeles train station, an art deco palace. The chandeliers are as big as cities, held by iron rope to a cracked ceiling. The ceilings are fifty feet high; the room would have made a good aviary. I sit in one of the brown leather-bound mahogany chairs. The wall clocks have geometric faces. The bronze hands never move.

I spend most of the two days on the train trip getting high. I had scotch in the morning as we passed through the snow-capped Rockies. I shoot up coke in the bathrooms on the first level. When I get stoned, I have to blow the smoke into the vents, so it won't seep under the door. I gaze at the silver metal walls, the miniature sink, and thumb-size soap.

With the buckle slapped against my left arm, shoes untied, and mouth and veins open wide, I take the stranger liquid in, the way I took my father. I earn my next high with this body, this sublimation for a high.

Hungry for a high my diminishing supply can't assure, I hunt these men down on the train, looking for the ones who will trade me drugs for sex. For once I am no longer my father's victim. I look at a man with a gold watch and fine, thin hair, unhappy. I find one. My mouth is dry, my arms rejecting the needle, the wrist limp, wanting it to be over fast.

I watch his gold watch as he shoots me up with my private needle, never shared: the gold ridges, black face, diamonds around the outlining circle of the watch, on the arm of the stranger, and the stranger holding his chin up as he did things to my arm. I focus on the man's white cuffs with initials sewn in blue thread on the apex. Could it be L.G.H? Or was it G.R.H. in tiny scroll?

I walk over to the miniature sink after the man leaves, taking out the small tube of mint toothpaste, washing in circles around my teeth, inside the gums, adding mouthwash, desperately trying to get out the odor of throw-up, the man with the gold watch and main line.

Afterward I walk down the corridors of the train, almost coffinlike. With this past stuff in me, I don't feel the distance is impossible. I somehow conquer time.

I would see my father in twelve hours. Could I tell him about the stranger on the train? Would I mention my body under a sink, on the bottom floor of a train, somewhere in the middle of Missouri, crossing the Mississippi River?

On the train, I try to interpret my father. I walk like him. I put my voice an octave lower. My shoulders and arms I spread wide apart to suggest a football player's width. I wear his black leather penny loafers. I even get drunk.

My father never taught me football. He wanted me to be a boxer. Late at night, he took me out to the garage. I placed my hands into his palms and he would wrap my arms in thin shreds of white cloth to protect my knuckles. My fingers were spread wide, and he twisted the fabric across my wrists and knuckles. I then lifted my arms wide into the air, turning them in circles. My father stood right behind me. When I got tired, he would hold my arms and raise them. Up and down for twenty minutes. The garage was dimly lit with a swinging red lightbulb. Its door closed. My father's clothes, Bibles, and books from Catholic school were stored around the garage in various sections. In boxes were his school journals, filled with pages of themes ordered by the rectors during Latin lessons. They had red marks all around the sentences with missed grammar and bad penmanship. Along the index were drawings of naked women with nuns' habits.

When I held these books, I could feel on my back the brisk floggings my father told me he would get from the prefect's cane.

The loving cups my mother clawed through in my bedroom are Notre Dame trophies that belong to my father. My father would give me these awards if I did things to him. This was my father's pious ritual with me.

"I'll give you this trophy," he would say, gesturing with his head, leaving the offer unfinished but clear.

My arms would reach down to his feet and slowly remove his black socks. His feet were cold and brown. Soft and burnt.

I had to unzip his pants. I would feel the cold ting of the zipper along my index fingers. They would shake. My whole body would go into convulsions. It took me ten minutes to get the zipper undone. I placed my hands into the folded opening of his pants. I had to keep my hands moving inside his pants for ten minutes until I felt a wetness on my fingers. My eyes were focused on his bare tan feet. These feet jumped when he got wet. The toes wiggled like little worms. Can I absolve my father for all these crooked deals we made on bodies?

This is what all the boys did at Notre Dame, he said.

The year I was five, I won twenty football trophies.

Tell me you love me, my father will ask.

44

I step off the platform and see my father walk slowly toward me.

I haven't seen my father in five years.

In the train station my father kisses me on the mouth, grabbing hold of my cheeks and face and thrusting his whole structure into my body. It is a kiss that is acceptable in public. He is reaching fifty years old, and I taste it on his lips, stingy with tobacco and scotch already settled in the throat for one hour. Father looks like a consumption patient. He doesn't look like my father anymore. The hero dead, he looks real.

A cigarette in his mouth. The unshaven face and throaty voice. The skin, not soft and brown but dry and chapped, the way it crept out of the jersey at his neck. Cold blisters along his forearms. And the sagging fat under his chin, a sign of age before his time.

"We're going to win this game," he tells me. "I'm standing on the fifty-yard line and the boys are huddled and I say, 'Go Irish.' My father's voice yells. "We're experiencing history, my son."

"Dad," I say cautiously.

"And the cheerleaders we've got lined up for after the game. I fuck each one. Up the ass."

He is stoned. I can tell. He is wearing mirrored glasses, but I can see through to the dilated pupils.

"They love it when I play with that little pearl of theirs for hours." He isn't really looking at me but at something he knows he did wrong, though he would rather play the game. "We can tag-team those girls. And we'll get you your own."

"It's not why I came here."

"Are we speaking English?" my father says, his voice belligerent. "We are in the middle of Notre Dame history and this is a part of your Irish roots." Father grabs his arms around me and begins squeezing tight. "You are watching your father make history for all the Irish boys who grow up watching Notre Dame games with their fathers. It's a rite of passage. Now you're a man. America and Notre Dame."

I look the other direction.

"What else could you come here for?" he says.

I don't answer.

He is wearing his Notre Dame pep rally shirt in blue and white and a blue hat with a gold-threaded *N* and *D* stitched across the brim. When he takes off his hat, his hair is gray at the tips and around the ears, but still full and black.

My father's body is unbalanced, intoxicated by the morning drinking. Usually by twelve noon it's five shots. And because I called him from the train to tell him I am coming, he must have done ten shots. He will hide this by walking very slowly and straightening his posture like a good actor.

Each movement seems to give him a pain in his right arm. And when he hugs me again, he is trying to apologize, squeezing hard against my ribcage, almost taking out the air. He holds me for long moments, pushing his whole chest into mine.

"Do you love me?" he asks.

I don't respond.

"Tell me you love me," he asks again.

"I love you," I say, my voice barely audible.

"Tell me again. Say I love you. A father needs to hear that."

"You know I love you."

"I need to hear it." His voice becomes agitated.

"I've already told you I love you."

"Is it so goddamn hard to say I love you?" My father's voice begins to boom across the hard echoes of the parking lot. "You know how much I love you," he says.

"I don't."

"Don't get sarcastic with me." Father cups my face in his palms. "I would take a bullet for you."

We walk through the station with his arm around me, my neck in his embrace, unable to let go. I know my face looks contorted, attempting to smile at his group of friends lined up by the car. I know the one who is his dealer, the ex-football quarterback who played for Notre Dame, and other people with no names. His friends that set up his drugs and orgies.

They all look smashed. When they meet me, the greetings are muffled, absent of small syllables that would give it meaning. "These are my best friends. The finest Irish Catholic boys in the Irish race," Father says.

I stare at the lineup, all five guys wearing dark mirrored glasses. I want to believe I am a part of this group. The only way to befriend these guys, I realize, is to expose myself to marijuana, coke, and anything pharamaceutical dropped into a mug of beer. I am waiting for the drugs in the car.

How much apathy would it take to be an assassin? How could I kill my father with the edge of a blade stuck into the spinal column? I could hold his palms up and slice the veins like a banana. I would peel the skin off. It would be three in the morning and I would have Strauss on. I like the idea of killing him to a waltz. I would have to hold his wrists inside the toilet bowl and flush, to wash the blood away. These are the thoughts that keep me alive and thinking in the company of my father. I try to monitor my desperation level, so it doen't overflow. I don't want to accidentally pull a trigger out of reflex.

I wedge myself into the car with some of the ex-football players and we drive to the pep rally, Notre Dame versus Michigan. It's not only the fall of God that makes people so desperate at Notre Dame; I factor in the regular human contradictions, the hidden abortions in the parking lots accompanied by the sound of the marching band, dressed in gold and blue, playing tambourines, trumpets, and drums, their feet stampeding throughout the arena. My father passes out in the car before the event, his arm lank around my shoulder, as one of the other men drives, manic and hyper at the prospect of the game and the arrival of the coach's son, the next of kin at Notre Dame.

At the rally in the arena, I sit next to my father, now revived, in the front row. Longtime admirers wait in line to receive his blessing, people my father tells me are grandfathers with their grandsons who grow up initiated into manhood watching Notre Dame games. I see him give a twenty-year-old girl his telephone number below his signature. They tell him how young he looks, how good he coaches, how they grew up watching him; nobody represents Notre Dame better. My father looks at me and laughs. I remind him of the glaring omissions in the newspaper profiles, when Father never mentioned me. Behind me, my father's friends exchange words: nigger, wop, kike; speed, coke, and hash.

I will call my mother. I will tell her I am alive.

Suddenly the lights in the arena fall into blackness and a trumpet sounds, as the Notre Dame marching band begins slowly parading through the tunnel, followed by a football team weighing two tons. Blue and white spotlights trace the open arena.

In the dark, I hear the pounding feet tread hard on the platforms and concrete aisles. High-pitched screams with coyote howls and a stampede from the audience, I'm braced to see a god appear.

45

At 4 A.M. that morning in my father's house I find a phone and call Grandma, gently lifting the receiver to avoid suspicious sounds. She is calm. We talk in whispers in between the lightning outside.

"How are you feeling?" I ask.

"I'm fine."

"How's your pulse?"

"Low."

"I'm coming home soon."

"They're looking for you."

"Don't tell them where I am."

"I told them to go to hell," Grandma says. "When are you coming home?"

"Soon as everything is finished."

"What needs to be finished?"

"Everything." I say.

"Does he have a gun?" she asks.

"Yes," I told her.

I know my father keeps the barrel of his rifle loaded. I think maybe they might shoot me in the T.V. room, as they watch a football game. A fifty-yard-dash bullet.

"He's never cared about anybody but himself," Grandma says. "Get out of there!"

"I'm not able to leave," I tell Grandma.

"What do you want to tell your father?" she asks.

"Everything I know about him."

"What do you know about him?" Grandma asks.

46

"First, I know how hard you drink," I tell my father the next afternoon, sitting on a park bench outside Notre Dame's gates with my suitcases by my side.

"I don't drink that much. I like to have a little beer," he says. "I like the taste." My father is eating Japanese food with various fish dishes he has laid out on the bench. "Have some of the udon noodles."

"I've lost my appetite."

"You need some food before your trip."

I watch him arrange the food and start mixing the jasmine rice, alfalfa sprouts, and salmon sushi on his plate.

"I know you are drunk and stoned from morning until night," I tell him. "Not including the various orange pill bottles in your dresser drawers." I lean in closer on the bench. "And a doctor's prescription pad on your desk."

"I have arthritis. And lately I have had the flu." My father is finishing the assorted vegetables on his plate. "It's much easier making your own prescriptions."

I start to get restless on the bench.

"Look how you're sitting and staring at me," he says. "Full of resentment."

"I know you fucked up my life," I say.

"Oh, yeah?"

"The nights in Malibu, in the movie theaters, and in your basement."

"We were just playing around," my father tells me. "You can't take that seriously."

I look at his face bloated from liqour, the eyes swelling, and how all the words come out slurred in between the saki and the sushi.

"Don't blame me," my father says. "We've all had fucked-up parents." My father moves his eyes up to the sky. "We've all been fucked by our parents." He then says, "I've gotta get a beer."

"Are we speaking English?"

"What else do you know?" he asks.

"Twenty things," I say.

This is the scene I always imagined for my father and me—discussing what I know about him and he continues to know less about me. The scene in my mind was as cold as today, 30 degrees, overcast, with Michelangelo clouds.

"I contemplated dusting you," I say.

My father starts to utter some response in a nervous pitch as I tell him, "Don't worry, I have no weapons." I reach over and grab my suitcase and pull it between my legs and get up. "It takes too long to escape from your parents," I tell him. "Sometimes it's suicide or junk. Somtimes it's just leaving."

"I never said I'd win Father of the Year," he tells me. "This is what you got." My father holds my hands tight in his; he is frozen, but sorting out the images in his thoughts. I can see his eyes get wet, little wet spots forming on his eyelids. This time he cries for real.

I pull my hands out of his grip. I pick up the suitcase off the grass and hold it in midair.

"I realize growing up without a real father, I was damaged," I tell my father. "I was tripped at the beginning. I have to go," I tell him as I walk away.

"But nobody has touched the oysters," he says.

47

"Lullaby of Broadway" is playing on the speakers on the train back to California.

I am sitting in the smoking car of the *Zephyr*. The smoking section is for the rebels of the train. We are up in front, so we would be crushed first in a crash. For ashtrays we make little bowls with tinfoil. The red wool curtains smell of sour hard candy and match the blue vinyl seats. We are passing cities with gigantic crosses lit by a thousand white lights. New Orleans is a day behind us. It took a whole day to cross Texas, and all I saw were crosses nailed to red mineral cliffs and the border to Mexico in a distant blue light.

If you walk on this train long enough you can get acquainted with anybody; it's like body cavity search. Farther west is where the people open up. A girl sits down next to me. She lays her maroon Bible and gold leaf papers across the table. She wears purple nail polish and little gold rings with snakes on them. Her hair is combed straight.

"I'm not particularly fond of the church," I tell her.

"Then you're damned." She starts to light her Carltons.

"What's your name?" I ask, blowing smoke into her skeleton face. Bones sticking out of her back. Her pupils like needles.

"Penny," she says. "Like the coin." She puffs hard. "Do you believe in God?" she asks.

"The concept of God had been distant since my trip to Notre Dame," I say. "I believe in self-will, I believe in Nietzsche, I believe in the facts. If I could be somewhere between the esoteric and God, I would be happy."

The girl does not respond. Her eyes stare through her glasses. She wears a knit sweater from the pueblos in Navajoland and turquoise jewelry and silver. She has reached 200 pounds and she is under twenty years old.

"What do you know about God?" I ask.

"He works in subtle ways," she tells me. "He's not melodramatic." She takes out her Bible. I could see the neon-green-highlighted Psalms.

"I saw God's face when I left my father," I say. "I have been saved." I look out the window of the smoking car. We are making our way through the edge of Texas into New Mexico, and there is no God in this place. I realize it all looks like a cancer out there, the shacks with boarded-up windows nailed in to protect themselves under a vacant sky, a diseased clapboard house, the ammonia on the mops, and the gigantic pampas grass.

48

I call my mother on the phone during a train break in New Mexico.

"Where are you?" she asks.

"In the Southwest," I tell her, while I stare at the mesas at sunset. The temperature is 30 and I watch my breath feeze in the air.

"Are you safe?"

"I'm coming home."

"Are you in danger?"

"Not anymore," I tell her.

"What happened?"

"I went to hell," I say.

"Are you stoned?"

"I'm spiritual," I tell her, grabbing the phone tighter in my hand.

I look at the cold dense air along the flat clear sky of New Mexico. My hair is brushed back by the cool wind. My eyes feel undilated. I can see between the lines of this life and the one I've left behind.

"Spirituality is for those who've gone to hell and come back."

49

I've been taking clonidine for kicking and an opiate blocker, naltrexone. I question how can you block good opium?

Grandma has no private insurance. My money has been put into trusts that the banks control because I am under eighteen. My grandmother refuses to take money from my mother or me. I go to the Hollywood Loan and Collateral Store on Vine Street, five blocks from Grandma's apartment. My mother has let me continue to live with Grandma after the Hollywood Boulevard suicide, maybe because she thinks being near Grandma will keep me from junk and knives.

I carry three sable coats and a fox, whose dead black eyes and nose I used to think could still be warm when Grandma draped it over her left shoulder.

I walk into the store, two days since my last hit on the train. All I see are people out of focus, their faces drained, almost stretched out, like the mirrors in a carnival fun house. There is an almost inaudible quality to their speech, like a tape recorder slowed down to a baritone drawl.

Inside the store is a harsh reflection of gold watches, typewriters, rifles, antique clocks. In the back I know they have a refrigerator for the furs.

The loan shark is a midget, Deborah. I know her from before. I have hocked things for drugs. She stands on a ladder behind the case of gold watches.

"We'll give you three hundred for the furs," she says.

"These are sable coats," I tell her. I dump all the furs onto the counter. The sable and fox ones. Even the green dyed sable.

"It's Christian Dior," I say. "Doesn't that matter?"

My palms are wet, my cotton T-shirt sticking to my back. Every move I make is a trip or a fall. My knees are limp, my calves unable to tense myself upright. Everybody's face looks like they are about to utter the words *speed, crack,* and *heroin* in a megaphone voice, deep into my ears. I lean heavily onto the glass case, almost my hand enough of a dead weight to crash through the glass and grab the gold watches. Pieces of glass slicing away the pain in my body.

I look into a brass mirror, propped in a case to be pawned off, and I see my face, yellowish, inflated, puffed at the corners of my cheeks and under my eyes. A slight green foam crusts at the corners of my mouth. My hair is greasy and standing straight up, short ends sticking out of the back of my head. I comb through my hair and find clumps of hair in my palms.

"I also need money to buy medicine to detox," I tell Deborah.

"Nobody wants furs anymore," Deborah says.

"Just when I want to go clean, nobody cares?" I say, my voice rising. "Everybody would prefer I stay high?" I reach over and start slamming my fist on the counter. "It's a conspiracy!"

I pick up the furs and throw them on the floor. I begin to step all over the sables. "I need money for my Grandma's experimental drugs." I don't know what else to say.

Deborah looks at me through a blank stare.

"Everybody knows the war is over. Everybody knows the good guys lost. Everybody knows . . .," I sing, belting out inside the pawn shop.

In the corner of my eye I see the security guards coming through the door.

After, they give me six hundred dollars.

I walk to Grandma's house, and even my shoes do not quite fit right. It is as if my feet grew an inch when I stopped shooting up. The soles of my black Converse sneakers are striped at the centers, my white socks protruding through to the cold outside the shoes' canvas.

On my way back home, I look at the gutter, my stomach churning, and then I lean over the curb on Vine Street and it comes first like someone was punching my stomach, the last week of highs speed out of my mouth and into the street. My arms are shaking after I lift my head up from the ground.

I remember the ballet dancers in the bathrooms when I was in the Los Angeles Ballet Company. Their bodies oiled, rosined, and powdered, they bent over the sinks and toilets, making direct points with their index fingers down their throat.

In the last two days of no heroin, I have remembered those days, when as a child I had a body, during those dried yellow afternoons dancing in the rehearsal warehouses, the skylights like a halo over the dancers and me on the varnished white bleached-wood floors. Back then I had more space. My hands didn't need to cover my mouth and chin the way they do now; my palm always fastened around my mouth.

I stand up and look at December around me, listening for my next move.

50

Grandma is physically unable to cook. She has ordered Meals on Wheels. The nuns of St. James Church deliver food to people homebound with AIDS or cancer.

The majority of the driver's list, she tells me, are past matinee idols dying of AIDS. They live in rundown brick tenements off Hollywood Boulevard. These are men from the fifties, their rent paid by the Actors Fund.

Each day Meals on Wheels comes at noon to Grandma's home, I open the door and thank the nuns, the two plastic dinner trays always prepared for three meals for Grandma to eat. The food consists of chicken cacciatore, green beans, potatoes, canned peaches, and two vanilla or strawberry formula shakes. They include a brown paper bag with an apple and jack cheese. Even though Grandma can get hungry, she refuses to eat the Meals on Wheels. The food piles up in the trash, a vapor of stale chicken and moldy sweet potatoes throughout the apartment.

"I don't want to die middle-class," Grandma said, once she saw what the bags contained.

Tightly positioned into the pillows, five piled high against the lime walls in pink rose pillowcases, Grandma sleeps most of the time sitting up, nodding back and forth, giving the impression of being awake. Her hair lies in braids down the side of the pink nylon nightgown. She is trying to sleep away the pain.

I take the formulas for myself, drinking them in the mornings, the strawberry taste on the top of the roof of my mouth suiting my cravings for sweets. I was feeding myself as I imagined my mother did with baby food, the mashed sweet potatoes and banana pudding. I want to be sober when Grandma dies.

In my pocket, I collect tiny silver-wrapped chocolate bars and cherry drops. In Grandma's kitchen tonight, my mother and I make batter for Swedish pancakes. Dropping the eggs on the skillet and watching the smooth thin batter begin to expand, the snap of the butter on heat, I ache for my teeth to be coated with sugar and strawberry syrup.

"I thought I'd never see you in the kitchen," I say.

"I was cooking you Cantonese Chinese food as a child," Mother tells me. "I've always been a good mother."

"Why did you stop cooking?"

"When did I stop?"

"After I hit puberty."

"Why didn't you cook for yourself?"

"That isn't the point," I say.

My bones ache from the medicine, with sweat along my back. I promise this is the last withdrawal.

"You disappeared," I say. "Where were you?"

"I was making money. I had to work in order for us to survive."

Mother begins to move boxes around and rearrange the living room. "I've never been a good enough mother for you," she says. "Too bad." Mother picks up large piles of coupons Grandma has saved and throws them into the trash. "I am not my son's keeper."

My mother stares at Grandma on the bed. She walks over and starts to shake her still body. "She could go unconcious," she says, holding Grandma's wrist up and checking her pulse. "It's low," she tells me, as her voice rises. "Mother?"

There is no movement. Grandma's arms are still. "She's not waking up." Mother begins to slap Grandma's face.

"What do you want?" Grandma says, her voice in haze. Her eyes slowly open.

"Don't do that."

"Do what?"

"You have to wake up when I tell you to."

"I'm not dead yet," Grandma says.

51

Tell me you love me.

I will not call my father, I decide, under the hot water spraying out of the shower head.

I'm taking a fifth shower. I stare at my arms burned red by the hot water marks. I want to wash these opiates out. I think it can be that simple.

After I get out of the shower, I sit wrapped up in a tight white floor-length towel. I reach for a cigarette. My hair is wet, full of soapsuds.

I think of the past two weeks, and that my only time alone is in a bathroom.

Later that night I go to Grace. Her skin is translucent, eyes blue, or green when she changes them with contacts. She wears the dresses she makes. Sometimes I see her in a royal blue taffeta dress with gold beads and threading stitched along the bodice.

We take a hotel room in Hollywood. She places madrigal music in my ears as we overlook the cityscape in its blue-gridded twilights.

She resembles Grandma's delicate sympathies, in the pictures of Grandma in the '20s, her arms curved and resting below her chin, holding her head up, able to look at me. Her fingers, slightly disjointed, have ink marks on the sides. The nails are missing, cut close to the skin, and she looks somewhat ravaged. She still carries with her the weight of another century. Like some countess in Europe, who was beaten and did not stay married for the title. She would have not. She has escaped from something. She allows her beauty to hang out without force or impurity.

"Do you love me?" Grace asks, lying in the motel bed.

"I spend time with you."

"For real." Grace sits half naked, up against the backboard of the bed.

"I don't know if I could ever be that way," I say, turning over in the bed. "It's not in my background."

"Is that all?" Grace asks. "Can't you do something about it?"

"I'll try," I say. "Do you want to get high?"

52

Grandma's bones are released into morphine on the Wednesday before Christmas. She sits in her brown leather movie chair, the red lamp dimmed, the phone disconnected, and we set the record of José Carreras on the player, closely placing the speakers throughout the room, placing them along the windows, hiding the sounds from the rest of the world.

We listen until midnight, when her eyes fail and she falls asleep, without the certainty of her next morning. My mother and I spend the days here, and I stay alone with Grandma at night while my mother does evening shoots.

On Christmas Eve I unlatch the large brown leather trunk that holds her opera records. I reach down deep in the trunk, letting the vinyl brush against my fingers, feeling the thin lines of each track. The records are alphabetized.

I pick out *L'Elisir d'amore* by Donizetti. I walk over to the record player and lay the fragile disk onto the felt turntable top. Pavarotti is playing Nemorino.

Next, I place *La Bohème* on the record player. I imagine Grandma and me poor and in Paris. I relate more to this opera. Enrico Caruso's voice moved me; he could hold a last note like a dying person's last request. Rodolfo's love for the dying Mimi reminds me of Grandma and me most of all. I can hold my own in every tune in the aria "Che Gelida Manina."

As I listen to the music, I can actually see Grandma dying, I see Grandma develop acute senses, her strength turning inward. Grandma has only her inner life.

In the bathroom, I take a scalding-hot shower, hoping to detox with sweat. It is my twelfth shower that day. Letting the steam rise through the air, I hold on to the railings in the bathtub, my arms draped over the curtains, my unclothed body and legs stretched out. The hot water comes down my back.

I think of the various bodies that have been inside me. I recount twenty things I know about my father.

Tell me you love me.

What twenty things do I know about the world?

My arms supple, my skin fresh, I place baby powder all around my body as if at some christening.

The morning light through Grandma's bathroom is silver. I sit along the rim of the tub, my legs crossed. I stare at the eleven-by-fourteen developed portraits of me hanging on the clothesline in the bathroom. It's the first time I see myself clearly.

I decide I will not call Father. Not even the next day.

53

My mother's Christmas tree is still lit at three in the afternoon. I sit in the wan light coming through my mother's bay window. The whole living room has japanned mahogany, the wood draped with ten yards of garland and red bows.

My mother has bought two gallons of red hot spice and sprayed the cinnamon liquid on couches, drapes, garland, Christmas tree, and lightbulbs, and today I watched her anoint her neckline.

In the center of the living room is a pink-frocked Christmas tree. The tree's long punctured pink stems reach out, holding gold bulbs by a thin wire.

On the brown tiled mantel is a gold-and-black menorah, with three blue candles placed snugly into the candle holders.

My mother is sitting alone, eating a pistachio ice cream sugar cone. I watch her from afar, and I can almost taste the cool ice and nuts; my mother's feet dangle off the wooden bench in the livingroom, suggesting a twelve-year-old girl, a sweet pleasure across her face. My mother the child again.

I go to sit close to her on the couch, feeling her body

removed, not in bitterness but in some halcyon cloud I can't understand. Her voice is high-pitched.

I sit on the couch with her for twenty minutes, not exchanging any words.

My mother's face becomes tense and all the joy is dispersed. Her pupils get wider and become a pool of tar. The first time I'd seen the wreckage across her face. The hours with the doctors, driving Grandma to the hospital, the junkie son.

A few seconds later, my mother takes out of her suitcase a gold box. Inside are her hand-painted baroque playing cards. She opens the lid and starts shuffling the deck.

"How do you play?" I ask.

I am dealt five cards.

"What's the prize?" I ask.

"My son."

"You have to win two games out of two," I demand.

"Game begins going in your direction." Mother deals the cards.

Mother places a five of spades in the main deck.

"I don't get it," I say.

"One card, for talking out of turn," she says.

Mother upbraids me with a two of hearts.

"What . . . how was I supposed to know?" I ask.

She slaps another card down on my deck. "Failure to say, 'Have a nice day.'"

A few minutes later my mother has won the game. She has no more cards left; she declares Mao.

"I'll be kinder next time."

"One of these days I'll win," I say.

Mother tucks the cards back in her pocket and returns to her pistachio ice cream, soft green melting down along the cone to her fingertips.

54

"Color is too upsetting for my eyes," Grandma says. "I may go into a coma." We concentrate on life before color.

Christmas night, Grandma and I enter the black-and-white world, sometimes sepia-toned because of the aged tint on the photographs from the sun, never in color.

Each photograph is clipped at the edges, pasted on black construction paper. The photos have bled at the sides, turning orange and red with age, and we avoid the distorted images. These pictures are like lost maps, leftover viruses under a microscope.

We drink red wine with the photos. Grandma lifts the glass to her sallow face, an ocher pigment, brown circles under her eyes. Her palms are a light shade of orange from all the raw carrot juice.

The pictures we look at have been taken before 1939, five-by-seven shots, Grandma on skis in the Swiss Alps, her lips thin and eyebrows penciled in with brown ink. She was in her early twenties, bobbed brunette hair, curls stapled to her cheeks, glued down with her own saliva and tobacco smoke.

Grandma's fingers hold each photo as if for the last time.

Grandma slowly becomes aware of her own time, the limited arrangement of segments, all placed like slides in a viewfinder. Her photos hang on the walls, as effigies, tiny medallions, snapshots of her history and Hollywood. It is like Versailles, where kings had wars painted in peace rooms, always reminding them of victory. In photos my grandmother and myself have a keen awareness of our own landscapes and work. These pictures document the fact that time has been captured, if only for one hundredth of a second.

"I had to win Mao." Grandma's voice is hoarse.

"Why?"

"That's when it was done to me, in Paris," Grandma told me. "I was starring in a play, *Le Bourgeois Getilhomme.*"

It was her first weekend away from home in Provence, opening in a play. The city that night had infinite exposures of light, with the smell of leather and tobacco burning against the harsh white lights of the river Seine. She moved among the high-voltage stage lights into the men who waited after the show for her, offering her diamond brooches, train trips to Istanbul, and a title.

That night, Grandma wore a strapless silver taffeta dress, her hair bobbed, the sixteen-year-old brown eyes under blue eye shadow, out to dinner with a talent scout from Hollywood. He said he would make her a star. Grandma leaned over the dinner table, balancing with her hands glasses of claret and Armagnac. Endives soaked in salt and vinegar, pigs' feet, stuffed hens, orange-marmalade duck, and crayfish.

Afterward they had strolled back through the Saint-Honoré quarter to the Ritz Hotel. Grandma walking in through the polished marble floors, into the lobby where the hotel's candelabras, clocks, and gilt were cleaned and polished five times a day. The hall porter in a black tailcoat grabbed the chance to light her cigarette before she sat down.

I imagined the room he took her to, a view over the Place Vendôme, the dim gas streetlamps seen through the curtains, Grandma at the half-drawn curtains staring at Colonne Vendôme in the square.

Then the black buckle falling, the patent leather shoes stepping over her small toes as she ran for the door. The long tear in her dress as she turned so quickly away from him. The falling gold phone, the side lamp crashing on the floor as he dragged her along, sweeping her body down against the carpet, up against the cabin trunks and hat box. Her arms tucked behind her and crushing them with her back. She screamed when he entered her, the hymen not even broken. He waits because it's too painful, so he rubs against her until it is safe again.

Afterward Grandma crouched over in the bathroom, her hands grabbing the pink marbled walls, turning on the massive chromium fittings over the bathtub, taking the water and monogrammed towels to wash her insides and her legs with hot water, the virgin maroon blood and semen dripping on the floor.

"That's why I could never tell your mother who her father really was," Grandma tells me.

Grandma tells me how she carried the baby from show to show, the blue carriage in the dressing room, lit by the overgrown lightbulbs on the mirror. The letters she never wrote home about the baby.

"I lost my daughter to Mao," Grandma says. Grandma stares at a picture of herself in a bistro in the Marais, Grandma wearing a large-brimmed hat with quail feathers, suggesting a character in a Comédie-Française play.

I see Grandma walking down Rue Saint-Honoré at dawn, passing the closed bistros, the flower vendors opening up their carts to an aroma of roses, violets, and lilies.

Grandma covered the ripped parts of the dress with a black wool trench coat, a broken heel in her left hand. She glanced at the Café de la Régence, thinking of Rousseau playing chess, the bisque dolls in the windows, the linen and lace shops a kind of solace. Grandma stared at her reflection in the glass window, realizing the necessity for imagination.

"My negatives. I'm leaving them to you. All the originals are in a gold metal box."

"What am I going to do with them?" I ask.

"Preserve them. They're worth a bundle. All the Marilyns, she's everywhere. You can do a mail order catalogue," Grandma says. "Don't spend all the money on drugs."

Later that night, I dye Grandma's hair. I turn on the tap in the washbasin and only the cold water comes out. Grandma says it is too cold. Her scalp would freeze. I place her weightless head into the washbasin and then apply the henna. Grandma screams even with the hot water. She cries through the dye process.

Before Grandma goes to bed, I comb and braid her hair. I close the shades. I leave the oven door open for heat.

While Grandma is sleeping, I go through her boxes of negatives. I am trying to find her lost negatives of Marlene Dietrich, Ramon Novarro, and Humphrey Bogart.

I hold small color transparencies in my hands. They are water damaged from the storage garage. I lift the one of Marlene Dietrich to the light. The colors have mixed with water and made rainbows along the image of Marlene Dietrich performing a song in Las Vegas. I can see Marlene is wearing a long yellow gown with a white feather boa and studded diamond rhinestone earrings.

In the photograph Grandma took of Clark Gable, he sits in a white tennis sweater with a script in his hand. I could look into his eyes and see the loss. I could smell the musk and the close shave, the salt tears in his eyes and the leather bomber jacket.

"I'm going to be alone when she dies," I say.

"Men are always alone," Gable replies.

Gable eats his raw steak and swallows pills for his heart, then grabs a tiny gold lighter and lights opium. "Opium is good for mourning," he says.

"I prefer to shoot it," I say.

Gable inhales the smoke in the air.

"Do you see the plane crashing?" I ask.

"I can feel the strands of her blond hair caught in the wind. At night I wake up and listen for the desert," Gable says. "I travel to the Nevada plains, trying to understand this type of nature, that flings you from heaven to earth."

Gable pulls out a stack of playing cards.

"Do you want to play Mao?" he asks.

"I'm just learning how."

"Keep playing," Gable says to me.

55

After 3 A.M. Grandma's pulse drops. I hold her limp wrists. I listen for the counts of death. I multiply two by twenty and think most of the time she dies and then comes back to life.

"Grandma, you have no pulse," I tell her tonight.

"I'll be fine," she says.

Grandma pulls the wool blanket over her head.

A few minutes later and she still hasn't moved. I shake her body and she gives no response. I start to slap her. She has no reaction.

I go to the record player and turn on Mozart's *Magic Flute* at the highest volume. I put the speakers next to Grandma's bed, one on each side of her head, and watch her motionless body surrounded by Mozart.

I dial 911.

I sit in the chair by her bed and wait for the paramedics.

56

I know someone is shaking me. I've woken up in a hospital. I am sleeping on a rollaway. It's dawn because the white sunrise is serene across my eyes.

A heavyset black nurse stands above me. I see her upside down. She moves from side to side of the bed. I see her through half-opened eyes.

"You have to wake up," the nurse says.

"What is it?" I ask.

"Your grandmother has expired," the nurse tells me.

"What do you mean *expired*?"

"She has passed away," the nurse says.

In the aftermath I stand next to Grandma on a stretcher covered with a cloth. I pick up a tag attached to the end of the stretcher. I read her name on the tag. I put my hand over the cloth. I continue to move my hands around the cloth.

57

After Grandma died, they had a therapist come and see me in her empty room.

They wanted to know how I've been.

I told them I've been shooting coke, got fired, contemplated dying, and have had sex with a mixed-up stripper during Grandma's slow death.

"Where do you meet these people?" he asks.

"Which one?" I answer.

"The most recent?"

"The man on the train?"

"Where do you go with them?"

"Bottom of trains."

They ask if it had something to do with my sexuality.

"It's over now because she died," I say.

"Is this the first time you've done these things?" he asks.

"No." I don't tell him the rest. "It's a game. Like my mother's cards," I tell him. "We play these cards so we can objectify each other."

The doctor passes me a little white cup with Valium inside and some water.

"I know what's happened," I tell the doctor. "I lost my

father and my grandmother in the same year."

I look past him, never answering his question. "Are we finished?"

"The pills will help you."

"I want to go see a movie," I say. "If a movie is playing, I'm inside the film." I look directly at the doctor. "And Grandma isn't dead," I say.

58

This morning, I sit in a limousine taking me to my grandma's funeral. Inside the car, I hold in my hands a dozen bovine lilacs that my father sent for the wake. They are tall green stems with almost full-blossomed heads. Lilacs are thornless, but when I touched them I scratched my hand.

When I was ten years old, my father would take me shopping for perfume. "I want you to smell of lilacs," he said.

Today, I sit at Grandma's funeral site. I can't remember the smell of lilacs. All I can think of are the macaroons and kugel. The idea is to eat and escape the pain.

I speculate about starvation. I could be re-creating the past in my stomach, the slip into coma and back out again.

Not unlike the pictures of Marilyn Monroe that Grandma had taken. Marilyn tried to kill herself eight times. It was because her hair wasn't blond enough. In one picture, Marilyn is reading a book of Rilke's poems. Her body is limber and bent, bearing the invisible marks from all the orphanages, from things they did to her in dark rooms. Maybe she died of sleeping pills and Pouilly Fuissé. These are the delicate suicidal signs of starvation.

Now I wonder if Grandma would believe in starvation

and suicide plans. I realize Grandma would never try to kill herself. Grandma's death would be to die of pears, figs, and tangerines.

The funeral has begun. And I haven't been paying attention. There's a black signpost nailed to a tree near Grandma's grave. It reads JEWISH SECTION. The cantor is singing away, two hundred people gathered. I stare at all the stout women in black. Their black patent-leather shoes reflected against the photographers' flashbulbs. Their dyed listless blonde hair in the wind. The old cheap smell of dime store perfume.

I'm Jewish for the first time. I will learn the rituals. I will sit shivah. On Yom Kippur, I'll remember Grandma with white candles in tiny glass jars. I understand filial piety.

Grandma wanted to be cremated, now she's under a pine tree in the shade. Some of the gravestones are built to look like buildings. One looks like the Sears Tower. Everybody that would visit these graves has already been buried.

The rain falls hard and hurries us, it's hailing as well. I think the hail could be Grandma's hard tears, the way it comes down in chips, as if for poker or gambling. It's a phenomenon of nature to be buried on the coldest day in the history of Los Angeles. Grandma had that kind of power.

Mother has people carry four different umbrellas for her. She wears a long sable under her raincoat. She wants to look elegant yet practical. Her white diamonds blend in perfectly with the rain. A gigantic mink hat from Russia covers her hair, with ear muffs in white rabbit fur.

Mother's cellular phone starts ringing. She gets up in a rush of sable and runs back to her car. The granite and her heels mix like a kind of shock treatment.

Now, the Kaddish is over. The pallbearers lower Grandma into the ground. She's in a maple casket. At the viewing I saw her wearing a green taffeta dress. Her hair was all made up, in curls. She looked beautiful, the days of the hospital behind her, and her eyes were closed, as if she were dreaming of somewhere else. Maybe she's back in Paris. Or the desert. This reminded me of when Grandma and I went swing dancing in Nevada; she taught me how to move.

"This is business," my mother says at Grandma's wake.

We are at Grandia Palace, a Greek restaurant. Grandma always loved this restaurant. There are over three hundred people here, and an orchestra. My mother managed to invite anyone who had ever met Grandma. Grandma hadn't wanted a party, or even a stone.

The restaurant is dressed in garish white fake marble and large replicas of the Venus de Milo and the David. The statues are made of a plaster that matches the fake marble and the blue trim. Running fountains are copious.

"Don't talk to anyone," Mother said as she arranged where everyone was to sit. "Save it for the camera."

Always rules. I don't sit with Mother, it's not right yet. Instead I find a phone booth, call the Deja Vu, and ask for Grace.

"I was supposed to go to Burma for a film," I find myself screaming. Suddenly, everything is too loud. A belly dancer followed me to the phone booth by the fountain.

"I can't hear you at all," she's screaming over the line. "Where are you?"

"My grandmother's funeral."

"I'm on next." I think I hear her say she's wearing a black G-string for the occasion. But before I can think about it too much, I hang up. I remember my grandmother saying, "Marry rich. And you'll be a star." And I think, *This is the day my grandmother died. This is the day I have to start life.*

I am sitting a long time, alone and wanting a shot.

I see my mother rise and stroll across the courtyard.

"You look pale," she says. She is nervous and doesn't realize she is starting to twist my thumb backward to emphasize her point. "She was my mother too," she says, leaning into me close, the way Grandma would. She is wearing Grandma's lilac perfume.

In my life with my mother I've had four sprained index fingers in splints. It's always the index finger that gets bruised. I have to learn how to hide my hands from my mother.

"Where should we go?" my mother asks.

"Somewhere in the middle of nowhere," I tell her.

"Let me get rid of the band," she says.

I go inside a back room that runs along a slant and realize all horizons are tipped from earthquakes.

I swallow two barbiturates. I am fifteen. This is the only way to get through the party.

The room is painted a cheap red, and I feel like I am on a movie set. *Just die,* I think. Then they could bury me on top of Grandma. The pictures of cows and barnyards on the walls mix well with the pills.

It's now I remember pawning Grandma's jewelry for drug money. How I took her diamond tennis bracelets and with an eyebrow tweezer picked out the stones. I detached them, sold them for nothing. I got one gram per diamond. Buying drugs with her jewelry was the best way to mourn.

I have my last dime bag with me in my flannel backpack when I go into my dance position, the way I learned when I was seven and performed in the *Nutcracker Suite.*

I go into second position and load up. Caress the syringe. Light a match over the spoon and then it's like flying carbon and all I can see is bronze and my eyes going red. I can cry now. I can imagine my father.

It's in the brown-dust-turned liquid, some link between father and son through a needle. I can taste his salt and the odor of that omnipresence. It's all cue card. I hear the roar of his voice in football stadiums and can see him everywhere, even in me, with my one good arm tied up in a tourniquet and his hands all over the rest of my body.

59

"Are you sober?" my mother asks.

"No," I say. "I'm just doing it until this part is over."

"This part?" my mother asks.

"The four-day mourning period," I say.

"That long?"

"How long does it take to mourn?" I ask.

My mother and I decide to leave the party and drive down Wilshire Boulevard.

My mother's face is scarred with tears, tiny drops of mascara staining her cheeks, the ends of the hair on the sides of her face wet and salty with the all-day mourning. She takes off her high heels in the car by the pedal, her black dress is hiked up; she is trying to come out of her body.

"It shouldn't take that long," Mother tells me.

I put my head out the window, the city brushing against my face, thin and transparent like a silk scarf.

"Where are we going?" I ask.

"I don't know," my mother says.

"Everytime I get in the car with you," I tell my mother, "we never know where we're going." I pull my head in from the outside. "We should plan things."

"That would be boring," my mother tells me. "Why do you do this junk?" Mother asks.

"It's good for ideas."

"I should try it."

"Heroin isn't something you try."

After the rainstorm during the burial, the sun has come out. We returned to the tropical sensibility that I learned growing up in Los Angeles. I know the winter of Los Angeles, with its blank expression of palm trees, stilled ocean, the refrigerated blueness of water. In winter, the water is blue and it is always blue until summer. Then it becomes a thousand broken pieces of glass, a suggestion of emeralds.

"I think we're heading east," I tell my mother, my pinpointed eyes taking the city in at a glance.

I decide this day is an Edward Hopper painting. I know Edward Hopper represents the singular. I relate to *Summer in the City*. A woman alone, drenched in the heat in the empty city, with just hints of a balmy breeze.

Everywhere in Los Angeles are remnants of the twenties. The streamlined design of buildings that Hopper captured. On Wilshire Boulevard these old buildings stand like phantoms. The May Company, with its twenties art deco decor, looks like an alien spaceship. It was one of the last neo-modern structures on Wilshire: seven stories of gold mosaic. Like Hopper's people, the towers remind me of my trips down Wilshire Boulevard and the complete isolation of a city.

I see my mother's Mercedes blur against the cheap mirrored office buildings that run down Wilshire. I can stare at myself the whole way down the boulevard because there is so much mirror and glass. Each block becomes an out-of-focus filmstrip.

If Grandma is listening, she would hear my suicide thoughts. She would hear that I want to jump out of this car going seventy, that my hand wants to reach for the door handle and let myself fly.

Maybe Grandma is an angel. If Grandma could touch me, she would feel my left arm reaching for a bottle of Dalmane out of the Wilshire air.

My mind wanders back to Grandma's dresses. The wind against my head feels like her purple chiffon from the fifties, locked in mothballs in her closet, whose long sleeves made of delicate fabrics that ripped with the wrong dance move could drape me like wings.

Now the dresses are in plastic bags, like a dead body. They are zipped up and airtight, smothered in the closet, each rabbit fur rotting away from the dense heat in her apartment, leaking holes and ripped insides. They all look like second-hand clothes, devoid of a beautiful body. Every night of spilled champagne has disappeared. I would have to give away all of Grandma's evenings in Europe at a garage sale.

"Our mother had brown toxic eyes," my mother says. "Nobody in Paris had a profile like her."

"Now she'll be dust," I say. Her whole death was like an opera singer's note, stretched out until the sound and air could not come out anymore. Some opera singers hold notes for entire minutes. It's the death of the voice, Grandma had told me. Now I know the absence of my grandma's sounds. This day becomes a vengeance on sound.

The prospect of Chinatown wavers before us, tucked below the hills of Silver Lake, no larger than two square miles wide, a tiny area that the police call "Uzi town."

I used to come here with Grandma. We would socialize with ancient men who smoked and shared their duck with us. They wore caps embroidered in silver threads and red satin and sat, as ex-prisoners of Mao Tse-tung.

There are open markets with racks of Asian pears, sweet fruit, and jellyfish. Roast duck in rotting three-week-old containers. Chicken feet and suckling pig. Salt splattered into the air from tanks of crabs and oysters. Barks and leaves and rows of ginseng used for medicine. Baskets of Kombucha tea. The mushroom plant used in tea for AIDS and cancer patients. They told me it would give Grandma a few more weeks. It's better than the chemo. I believed anything. Everybody gave me an opinion on how long the cancer would take.

"It's going to take a couple of weeks for her to decompose," Mother informs me.

"I thought it takes a couple of months."

"Maybe six weeks," Mother tells me. "After that she's just bones."

"Let's go to the beach." I ask.

My mother turns the car around and we drive to the beach. It takes an hour to get from Chinatown to Santa Monica. Sunset Boulevard stretches profanely like an Indian python all the way from Chinatown to the ocean. We will cross Echo Park, Hollywood, West LA, Beverly Hills, Holmby Hills, Bel Air, and Pacific Palisades, all via Sunset Boulevard.

Mother's '62 black Mercedes elapses through Los Angeles. She opens the black leather convertible top up to the setting sun. I hide from her the scabs on my right arm. I could inject bridges and lampposts into my arms. The openings under my scabs could fit my whole fist. I think, if I ate myself, what kind of high would it be? I would taste the radiation from Grandma's body and the chemotherapy. The fresh-squeezed carrot juice I made for her. The cotton lemon swabs I dripped across her lips when she couldn't eat anymore. The ice cubes for her sore throat. I've injected Grandma.

"Why are you driving so fast," I ask.

"I am hoping to get through the day quicker," Mother tells me.

We drive through Hollywood going seventy. My mother has taken a tape from Grandma's collection and plays Chet Baker.

Hollywood is weakly alive with its dank bars and green neon signs barely lit in the daylight. West of Hollywood, Sunset Boulevard ends on the naked bluffs facing the Pacific Ocean. What I see in the reflection of the water is a forbidden city painted in dark burgundy, lit by a side lamp, a laundromat life, nighthawks, and my grandmother's iris and lens.

We arrive at Wilshire and Ocean Avenue. This is the last street in Santa Monica before the drop below to the ocean. My mother and I get out of the car and my stomach aches from the heroin. We walk over to the park on top of the mountains that overlook the sea.

"I want to learn how to swim," my mother says.

"I thought you were afraid of deep ends?"

"Not anymore," she says.

"How do I learn?"

"I'll teach you," I say.

"I'm not swimming in that ocean," she says. "All the syringes and condoms."

Because it's January, the Santa Monica Pier is immaculate. The ferris wheel dips into gray clouds as if sipping champagne. The pier stretches its arms into shark waters, a long arm extended a mile off the coast, a home for plankton.

"Where do we go now?" Mother asks.

I start to get nauseous. "Home," I say.

"Where is that?"

"Grandma's."

I am thinking about all this as I walk to the cliff's edge. Then I think that maybe when you die you become even more connected to the ones on earth, that you develop a special physics of speech where you can talk and not be heard.

At the Pacific Ocean, I can feel her again as I stand in the dead redness of sunset. When I am near the ocean I become conscious. It's not just the salty air or powdered sand. My life begins by staring at water.

60

The next week, I wake up in Grandma's apartment. I had been kicking in her single bed in the bedroom where the walls have acute angles and the ceiling is so low it looms.

My mother has left a plate of Italian finger sandwiches, goat cheese, apples with potatoes from the party, and a large glass of fresh-squeezed orange juice on the table. In the corner of the silver tray is a tiny gift-wrapped box. I tear off the wrapping paper. Under the wrapping paper is my mother's gold container for her prized hand-painted baroque playing cards. A note is taped to the gold box. It says: *Mao at dusk*.

I contemplate if I will show up and play or find more brown dust on Santa Monica Boulevard.

I look around me at the boxes and file cabinets at each doorway of exit. The red Victorian lamp with red fringe on the ceiling. The black rotary phone off the hook, just like Grandma wanted.

I cannot see daylight because of the boarded-up windows. I see only tiny holes of light with dust in their projections. The light makes rectangular lines across the room, framing the dark places. I stand up and walk into the rectangular shape of light on the floor. The light is cool against my feet, with its yellow and white colors.

It's 5 P.M., and I plan to visit Grandma's grave. My mother has already had Grandma's stone put in place.

I walk over to her closet. Inside are all the gowns and dresses I will have to fold away and pack.

I walk over to the record player and put on the old thirty-three LPs of *La Bohème*. I walk across the room and move with the beginning of "Che Gelida Manina."

I brought twelve boxes. Each one is vacant, its giant lid opened.

In the second closet are metal file cabinets all filled with original negatives, color transparencies, and black-and-white proof sheets. Nothing is alphabetized.

Slowly, I walk up to the dead flowers from Grandma's funeral hanging upside down on the walls. They hang like trophies across the interior of my bedroom. Yellow roses, tiny and dried out, leaves with jaundice and mold. My room smells like an empty funeral parlor.

In Grandma's kitchen I left the stove on and the door open for heat. Now I turn off the oven and look at the empty tinfoil pie dishes next to Grandma's carving knife for her apples.

In the mirror above the sink is my face, scratched red with my fingernail marks, black circles under eyes not dilated.

Grandma taped a picture of Frances Farmer above her butcher block. With her gilded blond hair and tight silver sequined gown, she looks unsure of glamour, asking for Seattle, wanting to escape the aerosol spray on her hair and the cheap studio lipstick. Her tears surface in the makeup.

This I what I am, a week clean.

I return to the Hollywood Cemetery Park. I bring with me, in tinfoil, three tulips from the Hollywood Roosevelt Hotel.

Already Grandma's pink granite stone has been vandalized. One of the marble vases has been stolen. I take my sweater off and polish the edges of the gravestone.

The stone reads, *Beloved daughter, mother and grandmother. Artist, intellect, humanitarian. Died January 6.* There is no birth date on the stone. Grandma had a different age on each license and passport.

The stone, designed by my mother, has a bronze case on the outside. Inside is a reproduction of a five-by-six etching of Grandma in profile, behind a glass frame. It was taken from a sketch of her done in Paris just before the war.

The profile suggests a rare Victorian cameo. The image has turned pink with age. The sketch artist has drawn her auburn eyes with blue eye shadow. Grandma has brown hair in marcelled waves that gently tip down to her long neck.

Today, I look at the landscape near her grave. It's dusk, and the California sun is putting a scarlet light over the sky. This sunset is the portrait of my grandmother and me.

61

An hour later at the cemetery, sitting in the waning light, I see the headlights of my mother's black limousine pull up. Mother walks up to me by the grave.

"I knew you would be here," she says.

"I live here," I tell her.

My mother walks over to Grandma's stone. "Do you like it?" she asks.

"It's very pink," I say.

I take the playing cards my mother gave me out of my pocket. "Do you want to play Mao?" I ask my mother.

"What's the prize?" She looks at me suspiciously.

"Forgiveness," I tell her.

"I'll win this game," she says.

I cut the cards. I deal my mother a queen of hearts. The cards are placed on my grandmother's grave.

"Game begins going to the left," I say.